STITCH
IN THE
DITCH

A Quilters Club Mystery

STITCH
IN THE
DITCH

A Quilters Club Mystery

MARJORY SORRELL
ROCKWELL

ABSOLUTELY AMAZING eBOOKS

ABSOLUTELY AMAZING eBOOKS

"Perhaps thee will best understand what Abigail is like if I tell thee that when she quilts she prefers to stitch in the ditch, hiding her poor stitches in the seams between the blocks."

- Tracy Chevalier, *The Last Runaway*

Quilters Club Mysteries
By Marjory Sorrell Rockwell

A Christmas Quit (Prequel)

The Quilters Club Quartet

The Quilters Club Trio

The Underhanded Stitch

The Patchwork Puzzler

Coming Unraveled

Hemmed In

Sewed Up Tight

All Tangled Up

Needled

Stitch In Time

Cross Stitch

Fat Quarters

Available from
AbsolutelyAmazingEbooks.com

STITCH
IN THE
DITCH

A Quilters Club Mystery

Table of Contents

Part 1

"Potawatomi people lived off the land for over 9,000 years, but you'd need someone with a doctorate in Anthropology to find traces of them."

- Johnny Flynn, a Potawatomi native

Chapter One
An Indian Mound

Maddy Madison didn't know an Indian mound from a mole hill, but Indiana and Ohio are scattered with them – perhaps the most famous being the Great Serpent Mound in southern Ohio.

The Serpent Mound has been called a "Great Wonder of the Ancient World" by *National Geographic*. This 1,348-long earthen depiction of a snake is what's known as an effigy mound. Meaning it's shaped like an animal. Radiocarbon dating suggests that the mound was built around 300 BC by an indigenous people categorized as the Early Woodlands Culture.

They were perhaps a precursor to the Potawatomi. The Potawatomi occupied a big encampment near the Wabash River before being shipped westward by the US militia following the Treaty of 1833. This relocation has been called The Trail of Death.

Maddy had never visited the Serpent Mound. She had little interest in archeology, her attention more focused on quilt making. She and three friends – six of them in all if you counted her two grandchildren – formed a local needlework society called the Quilters Club.

In addition to Maddy, the group consisted of Lizzie Ridenour, the fussy redhead who oversaw the new quilting museum; Cookie Brown, the brainy blonde in charge of the Caruthers Corners Historical Society; and

Bootsie Purdue, the pudgy no-nonsense brunette who headed up the sprawling no-kill animal shelter on the edge of town. Add two precocious kids, fifteen-year-old Agnes and thirteen-year-old N'yen, and you had quite a confab.

The Quilters Club would have had little interest in the new Indian mound discovered just north of town had it not been for the dead body found atop the bird-shaped pile of dirt and gravel.

What made it newsworthy is that the dead man was none other than Evers Alexander Gochnauer, the recently appointed police chief of Caruthers Corners.

~ ~ ~

The old police chief – Bootie's husband Jim Purdue – had retired a few months back and the Caruthers Corners Town Council appointed Deputy Evers Gochnauer to fill the position. It had been a toss-up between Evers and fellow deputy Pete Hitzer, but Evens won the Council's approval by one vote. His cousin Boyd Aitkens had been the tiebreaker.

So it goes with small-town politics.

However, Gochnauer lasted only three months before his untimely demise.

Upon the death of the new police chief, Mayor Mark Tidemore immediately called Jim Purdue back into service as acting police chief. His first task would be to solve the murder. Evers Gochnauer had been strangled, according to the coroner.

"Gotta do it," Jim Purdue told his wife.

Bootsie was irked because this meant they had to cancel the trip to Disney World with their best friends, Maddy and Beau.

Beauregard Hollingsworth Madison IV was a direct descendent of a Town Founder, one of those hardy pioneers who settled here in 1829. Madelyn Agnes Hoople Taylor Madison was founder of the Quilters Club, ca. 1999.

Bootsie Purdue and Maddy Madison – along with Cookie Bentley and Lizzie Ridenour – had been bestest of friends since high school. Their four families often vacationed together.

But duty trumped an annual visit to Mickey Mouse.

So, Jim pulled his old uniform out of the closet, put it on, and strapped on his utility belt, complete with holster, radio, handcuffs, and baton. He extracted a .38 Smith & Wesson from his gun safe and loaded it. Then he found the discarded silver badge in a kitchen drawer and pinned it to his blouse. "Where's my cap?" he asked his wife, looking for something to cover his balding dome. At 60, his hair was less and his paunch more.

"On the closet shelf," Bootsie sighed as she dialed Maddy to give her the bad news about Disney World.

Chapter Two
The Return of Chief Purdue

*C*aruthers Corners – pop. 3,312 – couldn't afford a full-time coroner, so a local physician provided his services on a piecemeal basis. The office of Franklin D. Medford MD was conveniently located next door to Yost & Yost Mortuary. That's where he examined the corpse found on the effigy mound at Injun Woods.

"You sure it's murder?" asked Acting Chief Purdue.

"Pretty sure. Suicide by strangulation is rare. Usually that involves hanging. But your deputy—"

"– the Chief of Police, you mean."

"Yeah, Evers – he was strangled with a ligature, not a noose. You can see the marks on his neck. Here's the typical presence of bruising or ecchymoses about the marks, as well as hemorrhages under the skin and in the tissues around the trachea and larynx."

"Yeah, I see the marks –"

Doc Medford continued. "The telling part is fingernail marks from the victim attempting to remove the ligature. I found his own skin under the fingernails."

"He fought back?"

"Looks like it, judging from the bruises on his body. There's a big contusion on the back of his head, but it wasn't the cause of death."

"Any idea what was used to strangle him?"

"The marks are too prominent to be a soft ligature like a scarf. And a wire would have cut into the skin deeper. So I'd say a rope."

"Can you be sure?"

"Hold on, let me get out my magnification glass," replied the part-time coroner. He poked around in a drawer and came up with a 10x magnifier. Peering through a thick circular lens, his brown eye looked preternaturally large. He closely examined the dead man's neck, millimeter by millimeter. Then he used a pair of tweezers to extract a tiny fiber.

"You look like Sherlock Holmes," laughed Jim Purdue. "You only need a calabash pipe and s deerstalker hat."

"Gave up smoking. Heard it was bad for you."

"You gonna listen to the Surgeon General? He's neither a surgeon nor a general."

"Hang on a moment," said Doc Medford gruffly, ignoring the frivolous comments. He placed the fiber under a microscope, fiddled with a focusing nob, then said, "Here we are. I'd say the ligature was a cord made from *Abutilon theophrasti*."

"From what?"

"Velvetleaf. It's also called Indian Mallow. This is a common fiber used by North American Natives. It was introduced from China around 1750."

"How do you know this?"

"I've seen this fiber plenty of times before. I worked at Chicago's Field Museum while putting myself through med school. Northwestern University. Go Wildcats!"

"You're saying Indians made rope from this *Abutilon* whatchamacallit?"

"Absolutely. A simple process: You anchor two lengths of fibers to a post and tightly twist each length in turn to the right. Then the right-most twisted length is passed over the left length. The process is repeated, twisting the individual lengths, and then crossing the lengths over each other, splicing in new lengths of fiber to get the desired length."

"How do you know so much about Indian rope making?"

"Like I said, I worked on Field Museum exhibits. That – and reading Hilary Stewart's 1984 book, *Cedar*. In it, she gives a detailed description of traditional rope making used by Native Americans."

"So you're saying an Indian killed Evers?"

"I'm saying somebody killed him with an Indian-made rope."

~ ~ ~

"Welcome back, Chief," said Pete Hitzer. Petie and Viola Fahrner were fulltime deputies. Six others worked part-time. Add dispatchers Myrtle Dobbler and her sister Elvina, you had the entirety of the Caruthers Corners Police Department. Not big, but fact was the town didn't have much crime.

Other than an occasional murder. Like Evers Gochnauer.

"I hate being back under these circumstances," muttered Jim Purdue, hanging his cap on the coatrack in his old office. He noticed that the new chief had rearranged the furniture. Doggone, he hated that. Jim was a creature of habit. He'd get Petie to help him move everything back into place when they had a spare minute.

"What did Doc Medford say?" asked Petie.

Jim Purdue glanced up. "Said an Indian did it."

"You mean a Native American?"

"Whatever," shrugged the Chief. This PC stuff drove him nuts.

Petie wrinkled his brow. He was a skinny *Toy Story*'s Woodie kind of guy, all arms and legs. "How does Doc figure that it was a Native American? Is it 'cause Evers was killed up there in Injun Woods?"

"No, because he was strangled with a rope made of *Abutilon* something-or-other. A type of rope Indians make."

"D'you mean Velvetleaf? *Abutilon theophrasti*. is its scientific name."

"Yeah. How do you know this stuff?"

"Learned about making rope when I was in the Sons of Anthony Wayne. You know, the camper organization."

"You were in the Badger Patrol?" That was the local troop.

"Of course. Most guys 'round here belonged when they were twelve or so."

"I didn't."

"SAW's only been around for forty years, Chief. You're too old to have belonged."

"Thanks for that observation," grumbled Jim Purdue, rubbing his slick dome. Thinking back to when he'd had a luxurious head of hair. Jet-black, combed into a ducktail. Yeah, he'd been young once.

"Just saying," Petie offered a halfway apology.

"Back to the subject at hand," sniffed the Chief. "You're saying that every guy in this town who's between twelve and fifty-two knows how to make Indian rope?"

"That's about it. Besides, there ain't no real Indians in this town. Except for Matea Davis."

"You mean the watchman out at the Industrial Park?"

"Yeah, Matea's a genuine Potawatomi. Grew up on a rez in Oklahoma or somewhere out West. But his ancestors came from here. He's been teaching woodlore to the Badger Patrol."

"Guess I better go see 'im."

"D'you think he killed Evers?"

"Dunno. But somebody did."

Chapter Three

A Dead Body

Turns out, Maddy's grandson helped find the body. N'yen Madison had gone camping that weekend with the Badger Patrol, a local branch of the Sons of Anthony Wayne. SAW was a statewide camper organization similar to the Boy Scouts. N'yen held the rank of Lieutenant Colonel, a lofty position for a thirteen-year-old boy.

N'yen had been living with his Grammy and Grampy since his parents split up. But now Bill and Kathy were getting back together and they were coming down to Caruthers Corners next Thursday to pick up their adopted son. This outing with the Badger Patrol was a last hoorah for the young Vietnamese boy.

Maddy and her husband Beau were heartbroken, but they put on a brave face as they congratulated their son Bill on salvaging his marriage with Kathy. They had been apart for more than a year.

N'yen wrestled with conflicting emotions. The boy loved his parents, but he'd been very happy living with his grandparents. Their house on Melon Pickers Row was located only a couple of blocks from his favorite cousin, Agnes Tidemore.

Aggie was two years older, but N'yen had been promoted to her grade since he was a certified genius. They walked to and from school together, although lately she'd been spending more time with her new boyfriend, a kid named Bobby Elwood.

Stitch in the Ditch

At 5-foot-2, Aggie was budding into young womanhood. With her Alice-in-Wonderland blonde hair and sky-blue eyes, she was going to be a beauty. Her parents let her wear lipstick now, which made her look quite grownup.

N'yen didn't particularly like it that Aggie and Bobby wouldn't let him go to the movies with them. But, in turn, Aggie complained that the Badger Patrol didn't accept girls. She would have enjoyed going camping on that tract of land at the north end of the county known as Injun Woods.

Injun Woods had been in the hands of the Wayne family for 180 years. Posted with NO TRESPASSING signs and surrounded by a rusty 6-foot-tall barbed-wire fence, few people had ever set foot on the property. However, when 87-year-old Elmer Jackson Wayne passed away a few months ago (an allergic reaction to a bee sting), he'd left Injun Woods in his will to the Sons of Anthony Wayne. Old Elmer counted himself a distant cousin of Major General "Mad Anthony" Wayne, the Revolutionary War hero who served as the organization's namesake.

As troop leader, Ben Bentley took the twelve members of the Badger Patrol on monthly camping trips. The destination was often Gruesome Gorge State Park or the "back forty" at Old MacDonald's Dairy. This weekend was the Badger Patrol's very first outing at Injun Woods.

Everybody knew the name was politically incorrect. Maddy Madison preferred calling them Native Americans. Being a historian, Cookie Bentley went with Indigenous Americans. Lizzie Ridenour and

Bootsie Purdue were okay with Indians, even if it was a misnomer bestowed by Christopher Columbus, an explorer who mistakenly thought he'd reached the exotic shores of India. But nobody these days used Injun, a term that had faded away with black-and-white cowboy movies.

The area called Injun Woods had been on the plat maps at the Town Hall since the early 1800s. Nobody paid much attention to this pejorative held over from times past. Elmer Jackson Wayne had inherited the name along with the land.

Ol' Elmer had lived down near Flynn's Texaco on Highway 21. A white two-bedroom frame house with a falling-down porch. He'd been a recluse, never seen in town. Out of sight, out of mind.

Being a self-sufficient man, he kept an apiary on a hillside near his house. One day the mailman spotted the old man's body next to a line of beehives. Apparently, he'd been collecting honey when his bees turned on him.

As Winnie the Pooh said, "The only reason for being a bee that I know of is making honey ... and the only reason for making honey is so as I can eat it." Well, sometimes you get the honey, sometimes the bees get you.

~ ~ ~

Thanks to Elmer Jackson Wayne's estate lawyer, Ben Bentley had been given a key that unlocked the metal gate. An old wagon trail cut through the woods. The Badger Patrol hiked down the rutted trail looking for a clearing where they could set up camp. About midway they came upon an open space where the trees were farther apart. They pitched their pup tents near a plateau of land, then wandered around, exploring the surrounding wilderness. The hillock seemed to be odd-shaped, kind of like a bird. A curving ledge stuck out like "wings," with a beaked "head" on one side and a wide "tail" on the other.

"What's that?" asked one of the kids.

"Hmm," said Ben Bentley. "Looks to me like an effigy mound." Married to the executive director of the Historical Society, he knew about such things. Cookie had showed him pictures of various mounds shaped like birds and bears and deer and even a big snake.

"You mean an Indian Mound?" asked Buddy Smyth, one of the campers.

"That's right," nodded Ben Bentley. "Artificial earthworks created by pre-Columbian indigenous people. Some of these mounds were burial sites. Others were used for ceremonial or commemorative purposes."

"Indigenous people?" queried Georgie Yager, a sickly kid whose mother fussed over him like a croupy baby chick. She'd almost vetoed him going on this weekend's camping trip.

"That means the first inhabitants of a region. Indians are called indigenous people because they lived here before white settlers came."

"You mean before the Town Founders?" asked another kid, examining the prominence that had been identified as an Indian Mound. The earthen "bird" had a 20-foot wingspan, stretching beneath the low-hanging branches of leaves.

"Yes, the people who lived here before Col. Beauregard Madison, Jacob Caruthers, and Ferdinand Jinks showed up with their wagon train in 1829. Mr. Wayne's great-grandfather was one of the settlers on that wagon train. He donated this land to Sons of Anthony Wayne."

"So it's our land?" asked Georgie Yager.

"Kinda."

"Can we dig in there?" inquired Bobby Bjorn. "Maybe we'll find us an Indian skeleton and some pottery."

"Sorry," said Ben Bentley. "Indiana Code 14-21-1 provides protection for archaeological sites and historic burial sites regardless of their location on state or private lands. All archaeological sites with artifacts dating before December 31, 1870, are protected under this act."

"There probably is a skeleton inside this mound," said N'yen, demonstrating his brains-aplenty personality. "A recent study showed that nine out of ten effigy mounds are burial sites."

"What about that body down there?" asked Buddy Smyth. He was pointing toward the far end of the mound.

"Body?" said the troop leader.

"Yeah, you can see him there under those low tree limbs," nodded Buddy. "Is he an Indian?"

"N-no, I don't think so," sputtered Ben Bentley, climbing onto the flattened surface of the mound. He pushed aside the tree limbs to view a plump human form wearing a blue uniform. A policeman?

N'yen looked over Ben's shoulder. "Hey," he said. "That's the new police chief."

And that's how Evers Gochnauer's body came to be discovered.

Chapter Four
Quilters Club on the Case

As regular as an alarm clock, the Quilters Club met every Tuesday afternoon at the Hoople Quilting Heritage Museum. The facility had a large sewing room where the gals kept their fabric scraps, threads, needles, and other quilting paraphernalia. It was more convenient than the Hoosier State Recreational Center, where they used to get together. They had never liked sharing a room with members of that crazy macramé club.

As the person in charge of the quilting center, Lizzie Ridenour was master of her domain. Most folks considered Lizzie the best quilter in town, especially since two-time state champion Holly Eberhard moved to Bloomington. Lizzie had been tutoring Maddy's granddaughter in the intricacies of quilt making. Aggie was getting pretty good, had even won a couple of prizes in junior competitions.

Cookie Bentley was comfortable here too. The building – before remodeling – had been home of the Caruthers Corners Historical Society. But a year or so ago, the Historical Society had moved into a wing of the Perricock Museum of Science and History, that gabled stone mansion on a hill overlooking the town, allowing this building to be repurposed for the quilters.

Bootsie Purdue had recently taken on the presidency of the animal shelter, promptly adopting three dogs. She'd named them Inka, Dinka, and Doo, an homage to the old Jimmy Durante theme song. Inka was a black Doberman, Dinka was a blue-eyed Malamute, and Doo was a tiny Chihuahua. She and her husband Jim doted on them.

In addition to Aggie, Maddy Madison always brought along her grandson N'yen to the gatherings. This one might be his last. His parents would arrive day after tomorrow to retrieve him. Maddy's heart was breaking at the thought of him going back to Chicago.

As usual, N'yen took up station in a corner of the room and began playing Tower Duel on his iPad. A multiplayer tower defense game, he often pitted himself against an anonymous opponent known only as Beelzebub666.

"The Devil" – as N'yen called him – was winning again. N'yen was vexed. Who was this Beelzebub666? Had he in fact met his match?

At barely 5-foot-tall, the Asian boy was small for his age. That was exasperated by his skipping grades; all his classmates were older and more physically developed than him. He didn't mind being called "Peewee" and "Atom Ant," knowing that he was smarter than all of them put together. But the advantage of a stratospheric IQ was diminished when a total stranger could beat you at a stupid computer game.

His cousin Aggie wasn't very sympathetic. She thought he was "too big for his britches," a term he hadn't heard before. His trousers fit just fine, thank you very much. But Aggie was unmoved. She enjoyed seeing him taken down a peg by Beelzebub666.

"Be nice," admonished their grandmother. But Aggie and N'yen were more like siblings than cousins. Frenemies was an apt term.

Aggie sometimes brought along her dog Tige to the Quilters Club gatherings. He was a Heinz 57 mutt, a dubious mixture of wire-haired dachshund and various unknown varieties. Properly housebroken, Tige lay on the floor near Aggie's feet and chewed on a rubber bone while she sewed.

"So Jim is police chief again?" asked Lizzie. She'd heard about it from her husband Edgar. A retired bank president, he served on the Town Council. As did all their husbands.

"Yes, the Town Council brought Jim back to solve Evers Gochnauer's murder."

"So it *was* murder?" asked Maddy.

Bootsie nodded. "The coroner says he was strangled." As the police chief's wife she had an inside track on such information.

"That's what happened," confirmed Cookie. "Ben saw the ligature marks around his neck." Having found the body, her husband got an up-close look. He'd been having nightmares ever since. He and Evers had been on the same bowling team – the Gutter Boys – at Al's Alley over in Burpyville.

"What was Evers doing out there at Injun Woods?" probed Lizzie. An out-of-the-way spot, Elmer Jackson Wayne's barbed-wire fence had kept out visitors. The thick oak trees obscured it from an aerial view. No wonder folks hereabouts didn't know there was an old Indian mound on the property ... although the name might have been a clue.

Stitch in the Ditch

"Maybe Evers was checking out the new camping area for the Badger Patrol," suggested Bootsie.

"No, Ben would have known if he'd been doing that," said Cookie. "Evers would have had to get the gate key from Ben." Her husband held the rank of Brigadier General in the Sons of Anthony Wayne. There was talk about him becoming SAW's chief executive officer next year.

"Quite a mystery," mused Maddy, working on her quilt. She was sewing on the lower side of a seam, as close to the seam as possible – what's known as a Stitch in the Ditch. The technique covered up misplaced stitches. Stitching in the ditch is not often chosen by hand quilters, the method usually relying on a sewing machine. But Maddy was determined. Her hand was still a little shaky since that stroke a couple of years ago.

"Maybe Uncle Jim could use some help from the Quilters Club," posited fifteen-year-old Aggie Tidemore.

"Oh sure, he'd like that," laughed Bootsie. Meaning just the opposite.

The Quilters Club had a growing reputation as amateur sleuths. They had solved several local mysteries involving Lost Boys, Viking runes, hidden treasures, haunted mansions, Russian spies, and UFOs. All of these cases had more or less involved quilting know-how. But this one didn't seem to have anything to do with the needlecraft arts. Not yet.

Nevertheless, Maddy said, "Yes, we *should* look into this. We all knew Evers. He was a decent guy. His mother sings in the choir at the First Mennonite

Church. We shouldn't let some dirty-rotten killer get away with this."

And that was that.

~ ~ ~

Acting Police Chief Jim Purdue wasn't looking for any help from his wife's quilter pals. They were always sticking their noses into police business. In the past, Jim couldn't complain. Mayor Mark Tidemore had been his boss ... and Maddy was Mark's mother-in-law ... and Aggie was the mayor's daughter. Add to that, Bootsie being his wife. And Lizzie and Cookie were his buddies' wives. The deck was stacked against him. He'd had little choice but grin and bear it when the Quilters Club stepped in.

Sure, the gals had been successful in solving several local crimes. But he was sure he would've eventually nabbed the culprits if those busybodies hadn't got in the way.

Maybe he was being hard on them. But now he could afford to take a stand. The mayor couldn't fire a man who'd already retired!

Jim Purdue drove over to the Caruthers Corners Industrial Park and used his master key card to get inside the gated compound. He found Matea Davis watching a flickering 32-inch TV in the guard shack. The schedule required the night watchman to patrol the grounds every hour on the hour. The time being 8:37 p.m. by Jim's Zodiac ZMX-03 wristwatch, Matea was in the middle of a rerun of *Dancing with the Stars*, Season 9. He had a crush on Kelly Osbourne. He liked chubby girls.

"Hey, Chief Purdue," the young Potawatomi greeted his visitor. Standing to shake his hand. Always respectful of White People – *Cmokmanuk*, as he called them. "What brings you out here? ZapData's the only company that has anybody working this time of night."

"Came to see *you*."

"Does it have anything to do with Evers Gochnauer? Saw on TV you'd been called back to active duty to solve his murder."

"Oh? D'you know anything about it you should be telling me?"

Matea gave a wide toothy grin. He was both handsome and charming. No wonder everybody liked him. "If I did, you wouldn't have had to come to me. I would've come to you."

The Chief rubbed his chin, trying to decide how to begin. "Actually," he said, "I wanted to ask you about Indian rope making. Know anything about it?"

"A little. However, I prefer to buy nylon cord at Home Depot. Better tensile strength."

"Ever made rope out of Velvetleaf?"

"Sure, back when I was a kid. Velvetleaf, Swamp Milkweed, White Indian Hemp, Basswood, Cedar, you name it. Easy to make rope from any of them."

"Got any rope laying around now?"

"Chief, it sounds like you've got something in mind. Why are you interested in my rope making skills?"

"Evers Gochnauer was strangled with a rope made of Velvetleaf. I'm looking for someone who might have some."

"Go over to the Badger Patrol's clubhouse. They've been practicing their Indian handicrafts lately. They've got plenty of rope."

"Doubt a kid did it. As you'll recall, Evers was a hefty guy. Be hard for a twelve-year-old to overpower him."

"You think I did?"

"Well, you're the only Indian we have 'round here."

"I'm guilty of that, Chief. But I didn't choke Evers Gochnauer with a rope made from Velvetleaf. Although we always called it Indian Mallow back on the rez."

"Do you happen to have an alibi for Friday night?" The Badger Patrol had discovered the body on Saturday morning.

The 23-year-old Native American frowned. "Now you're hurting my feelings, Chief. I was working right here. After all, I'm the park's night watchman. You can check my timecards, if you want."

"Maybe I will."

"You want a suspect, look in your own shop."

That gave the acting police chief pause. "What d'you mean by that?" he demanded.

Matea hesitated, then said, "I hear Petie Hitzer was mighty disappointed at being passed over for your old job."

Chapter Five

Archeology 101

Although he was a paleontologist by training, Dr. Howard Carvel Oakman of the Perricock Museum of Science and History was dispatched to examine the newly discovered effigy mound at Injun Woods. He parked his dusty '07 Jeep Cherokee at the open gate and hiked into the thick woods, following the old wagon trail.

Wearing his battered brown fedora, Howie Oakman looked like a shorter version of Indiana Jones, a comparison he cultivated. All he needed was a bullwhip. But today he carried a leather case that held a Nikon D3200, a 20-foot tape measure, a pad of graph paper, and an Ingalls steel alloy hand pick.

When Howie came to an opening among the white oak and yellow poplar, he stopped to survey the surroundings. A few camo pup tents had been abandoned by the Badger Patrol, left to sag like a herd of brokeback horses. Backpacks and canteens and cooking pots lay scattered among the trees, evidence of their panic in finding a dead body.

Over to the left, under a canopy of cottonwood trees, he could see the humped shape of the Indian mound. Nearly hidden by branches bearing green triangular leaves, the mound's outline was partially obscured. All he could make out was a three-foot-high plateau covered with a patina of grass and moss.

Closer inspection revealed the bird-like contour of the earthen mound. While many Indian mounds were essentially flat-topped pyramids, simple conical mounds, or complex concentric circles, a number of ancient mounds took the shape of animals and birds.

These so-called effigy mounds were often burial sites containing one or more human remains. A survey of 586 sites, using ground-penetrating radar and magnetometry, revealed that 87 percent contained evidence of burials.

Most effigy mounds were built during the Late Woodlands Period (350 - 1300 CE). The Woodlands Culture was a loose affiliation of multiple tribes, connected by a common network of trade routes.

These mounds are still revered by First People who go there to speak to ancestors and give thanks. Although primarily visited by the Ho-chunk, whose ancestors likely built the great majority of the mounds, other indigenous nations such as Ojibwe, Potawatomi, Kikapu, Oneida, and Menominii are known to view them as sacred sites.

This particular bird mound showed no signs of having been disturbed; no digging, no excavation, no agricultural intrusion. Its isolation on this fenced-off tract of wooded land had protected it from looters.

One of Howie's duties at Perricock Museum was to act as liaison with Indiana's Division of Historic Preservation and Archaeology. Per state statute (Indiana Code 14-21-1-12), one of the mandates of the DHPA was to conduct a program of archaeological research and development.

According to a DHPA survey, Indiana has 1,183 pre-European-contact Native American earthwork sites that contain at least 2,100 individual mounds or constructs. However, no topological maps or surveys placed any Indian mounds in Caruthers County.

The most complete archeological survey of these earthworks is *Ancient Monuments of the Mississippi Valley* by Ephram G. Squier and Edwin H. Davis, published in 1848 by the Smithsonian Institution. Unfortunately, many of the mounds documented in this study have since been destroyed or diminished by farming and development. Archaeologists still refer to this existent record for identifying mound sites.

According to one estimate, more than 15,000 effigy mounds have been lost due to plowing, farming, and grading.

Housing developments have been a threat to mound sites too.

Ironically, archaeologists themselves are responsible for a large volume of destruction.

Examples:

- A large mound in New Castle was destroyed by Ball State University archaeologists.
- Indiana University archaeologists destroyed a 2,000-year-old mound in the Henge Complex of Mounds State Park near Anderson.
- Carter University diggers ruined a site near Terre Haute.

And municipal and government workers have done their share of damage, too.

- WPA workers excavated the Angel Mounds site in southwest Indiana, uncovering more than 2.5 million artifacts.
- Workers building a road in Mt. Vernon, Indiana, damaged an ancient burial mound, causing a treasure trove of silver and copper to pour from the ground.

No wonder people plundered Indian mounds!

Howie Oakman was known for his thorough reports, whether documenting *T. Rex* fossils or a pile of dirt left by ancient indigenous people. He took plenty of measurements and photographs, carefully recording this previously unknown site.

Slowly he circled around the mound making sketches and taking notes. The wingspan was precisely 22.3-feet across. From head to tail it measured 8.7-feet. The beak area had broken off, leaving a pile of grit and gravel. The tail was broad and flat. This effigy was small compared to some bird mounds; he knew of one with a wingspan of 260 feet!

He drew a "map," careful to get the proportions right. With the angled wingspan, it reminded him of a bird-shaped effigy mound he'd seen years ago at Observation Hill near Madison, Wisconsin. Birds accounted for the majority of animal-shaped mounds.

Checking out the flattened surface of the mound he observed a number of footprints, big and small. Most likely belonging to Badger Patrol campers and Caruthers Corners Fire Department paramedics. Any evidence of the murderer of Evers Gochnauer had been trampled underfoot. A completely defaced crime scene. That would certainly make the job harder for Chief Purdue.

Howie Oakman studied the scene for a moment. Bugs buzzed around his head like tiny kamikaze pilots. Smacking at them, he walked the length of the mound's surface. The insects sounded like static electricity. The ground beneath his feet felt pretty solid. Amazing how well it had withstood the elements over a span of some 2,000 years.

Standing there, he thought about the dead man – Police Chief Evers Gochnauer. Was it significant that the body had been found atop an Indian mound? Could the murder have been ceremonial? Did the location send some kind of arcane message? Or was its placement here merely a bizarre coincidence?

Howie climbed down to complete his examination of the surrounding area. Ignoring the nearby pup tents and abandoned backpacks, he focused on the parameter of the earthen structure. As he walked around the mound, his eye caught a flash among the decomposing oak and poplar leaves. Sunlight on metal. Bending down, he retrieved a police badge. Did Evers Gochnauer lose it in a struggle with his assailant?

He placed it in a plastic specimen bag, careful not to smear any potential fingerprints. If he hadn't become a paleontologist, he thought he might have made a great detective. He was an avid reader of mysteries. His favorites were stories based on forensic science by Patricia Cornwell, Kathy Reichs, and Lisa Black.

This mound was a great archeological find. Too bad it had to be discovered in this manner.

Chapter Six

The Investigation

Wednesday morning Maddy and her gal pals gathered at the Cozy Café to plan their investigation of Police Chief Gochnauer's death. A quartet of Agatha Christies huddled in a small-town diner. Not quite the elegant setting of an Orient Express dining car or the English country manor of Styles Court, but this obscure little corner of Indiana would do for the moment.

Cozy Café had started out as a converted railcar, but some years ago a squarish structure had been added onto the rear to expand its capacity. The exterior façade exhibited an archetypical stainless-steel siding, as did much of the shiny interior trim. A Formica counter stretched the entire width of the refurbished diner. In addition to counter service the diner offered six booths and a scattering of sturdy metal tables.

Squeezing into the corner booth, the four women filled it to capacity. Blame the crowding on Bootsie, who had gone off her diet. Having gained a quick 20 pounds, she was turning into a brunette blimp with a pixie haircut.

Aggie and N'yen were in school today, the first day of the new semester. N'yen was only going in to inform officials that he would be transferring back to his old school in Chicago. There was some debate whether or not Chicago would honor his advanced placement, a decision that had allowed the little brainiac to skip two grades. His IQ justified it, but his emotional level was still that of an immature thirteen-year-old.

Aggie was totally bummed that the Quilters Club was having a meeting without them – especially since it had to do with detective work. She liked quilt making, but solving a mystery was the most exciting thing in the whole wide world. "Too bad," her Grammy had said. "But education is more important. You can catch up on our investigation this weekend."

"Move over," grumbled Lizzie, hanging off the end of the booth's padded seating.

"I'm in as far as I can go," snapped Bootsie. She gave another push with her broad hips, but there was little give. The booth was packed as tight as college kids in a phone booth.

"You're crushing us," protested Cookie, trying to make more room. "You've got to get back on your diet, girlfriend."

"I was doing so good," whined Bootsie. "Then I ate a tub of watermelon ice cream. No matter how hard I tried, I just couldn't say no."

"What happened to your Weight Watchers Program?" asked Maddy. Caught in the corner, barely able to breathe.

"I just don't have the same will power as Marie Osmond," sighed Bootsie.

Maisie Walters rushed over with four coffee mugs, filled to the brim with freshly brewed Maxwell House. "Here you go," she trilled. "Drink your coffee. And I'll pull up a chair for Liz. That'll make you all more comfortable."

As it happened, Maisie was not only the proprietress of Cozy Café, she was Maddy's twin sister. Fraternal twins, in that they looked nothing alike. Maddy with her oval face and warm smile was a dead-ringer for actress Ellen Burstyn, while Maisie could easily pass as an older version of Flo, that frazzled woman in the Progressive TV commercials.

The two women hadn't known they were related until a couple of years ago. Turns out, Maddy and Maisie had been the secret love children of Herbert Hoople, one of the town's famous Hoople Quadruplets. As such, they had been adopted by different families, literally separated at birth. Now that they had been acknowledged by the Hoople estate, each of the sisters had received a humongous nine-figure trust fund. But other than satisfying philanthropic impulses, neither woman had changed her day-to-day lifestyle. Business as usual, Maisie still waited tables in her diner.

"Special this morning is watermelon oatmeal," Maisie announced. Caruthers Corners was known as "the watermelon capital of Indiana," that being the town's main agricultural product.

"Two bowls for me – with real cream," said Bootsie. "And plenty of sugar."

Lizzie wagged a finger, making her flaming red hair sway. "No, I'll have one of those two bowls. And make it with skim milk. No sugar."

"Phooey," frowned Bootsie, unhappy with this intervention.

"Oatmeal for me too," said Maddy.

"I'm not sure what I'll have," muttered Cookie, adjusting her glasses as she studied the menu.

"You know the menu by heart," Lizzie hissed under her breath. "After all, you have an eidetic memory."

"Oh, okay, a poached egg," the town historian decided.

"Grits?"

"No. A slice of watermelon on the side."

"You got it, hon," said Maisie and set off toward the diner's kitchen area, an orderly expanse of grills and microwaves and toasters and coffee urns behind the long white Formica counter.

"About our new case," Maddy took charge, "we need a strategy." She was the alpha member of the group, a natural leader. Her silver hair reminded you of a general's helmet.

"Right," everyone said in unison. They worked well together. Years of practice, ever since Maddy organized them into a sewing club in high school. A precursor of the Quilters Club.

"Divide and conquer," said Maddy. "Assigning a task for each of us will move things along faster."

Twenty minutes later, they had developed a plan of action.

It was as simple as 1-2-3-4:

1. Bootsie would pump her hubby for all the facts of the case.
2. Lizzie would call on Enid Gochnauer to find out any details about her son's last day.
3. Cookie would look into the history of Injun Woods, trying to determine who else had access to the property besides her hubby.

4. Maddy would talk with Myrtle Dobbler to get the police dispatcher's inside knowledge about any calls that Evers received on his last day. Then she would check them out, one by one.

"That should do it," pronounced Maddy, satisfied with the outlined course of action. They vowed to get on it right away.

"Aggie's going to be upset at being left out," said Lizzie. She'd self-appointed herself as the girl's mentor.

"I'll let her help me after school," Maddy promised. No way she could keep her precocious granddaughter from getting involved; she knew that from experience.

Satisfied, Lizzie said, "Let's find this killer. Evers deserves that. Nobody liked him much, but that was a terrible way for him to die."

"Evers was basically a good cop," said Bootsie, repeating her husband's words. "Sometimes he could be lazy and a bit of a bully, but Jim thought he'd make a good chief in spite of his shortcomings."

"May he rest in peace," said Cookie, a devout member of St. Paul's United Methodist Church.

"Amen," mumbled the others. Lizzie wasn't a big churchgoer, but she joined in nonetheless.

"Okay, that's it," said Maddy, drawing the meeting to a close. "I'll pick up the check. We'll meet up here at, say, four o'clock this afternoon."

"We can split the tab," offered Lizzie, reaching for her purse.

"I'll need change for a twenty," said Cookie.

"I've got money here somewhere," Bootsie pawed in her oversized handbag.

Stitch in the Ditch

"Off with all of you," Maisie shushed them along. "Today breakfast is my treat."

Ever since coming into a trust fund, Maisie had been given to random acts of generosity. Picking up a breakfast tab of $12.95 hardly broke the bank.

Chapter Seven

Looking for Clues

E nid Gochnauer was a dumpy woman, forty or fifty pounds overweight, her plump face surrounded by bright blue hair. She reminded you of Mama Smurf.

"My poor, poor boy," she cried on Lizzie Ridenour's shoulder when she showed up with a bouquet of flowers. A lovely selection of tulips from Personally Yours Flowers & Gifts.

"There, there," dutifully said Lizzie.

"I don't know what I'll do without Evers," the blue-haired woman wailed. "I'll never be able make it on my own. I've only got a small pension from when my husband got run over by a state mowing machine. I suppose I'll have to sell my home and move into an assisted living facility. I can't afford to keep the place without Evers' salary. I don't know what poor Tommy will do."

"Tommy?"

"Tommy Truehart, my nephew. He lives with Evers and me."

Enid's modest three-bedroom bungalow was located on 8th Avenue on the north side of town, a rundown area once known as Shantytown. Housing prices were low around here. She wouldn't be getting much of a retirement fund from the sale of this house, thought Maddy. But maybe her son's death benefit as a municipal employee would help a bit.

"Speaking of Evers, where was he supposed to be on the night he died?" Lizzie deftly changed the subject.

Mrs. Gochnauer let out an involuntary sob. "He didn't come home Friday night. He phoned to say he had a meeting with one of his deputies. I figured he and Petie were going out carousing. They did that sometimes."

~ ~ ~

Myrtle Dobbler loved the watermelon cookies Maddy brought to the station. She was already a few pounds overweight, the consequence of a desk job and too many potato chips and Pepsis. Maddy had timed her visit to avoid Jim Purdue and any of the deputies, knowing they would be tied up with an overturned Home Depot truck on Field Hand Road. She'd heard about it on the radio. That was a tricky curve for speeding vehicles.

"These cookies are very tasty," Myrtle thanked her benefactor. "What did I do to deserve them?"

"I baked a batch this morning. Had an extra dozen so my husband Beau suggested I bring them down here to share with the police. But I see you're the only one here."

"Don't worry, I'll share them. Well, some of them."

Maddy switched the subject: "Beau and I are so upset over Evers' death. I'm sure it must be hard on you to lose your chief."

"Yes, we was jus' getting used to our new working relationship, me reporting to him. It was such a shock when I heard he was dead."

"Do you remember your last conversation with him?"

"Sure. He told me he was leaving early. Said he had a meeting."

"Oh, a meeting with whom?"

"Didn't say. I told Petie at the time, Chief Gochnauer should keep me better informed. Chief Purdue did."

"So the meeting wasn't with Petie?" Lizzie had phoned her to report Enid Gochnauer's last conversation with her son.

Myrtle Dobbler sat back in her chair, a puzzled expression on her burnt-marshmallow face. "How could it have been with Petie? He was sitting right here, filling in for Viola."

"Who's that?"

"Viola Fahrner – she's the other deputy. Viola was out sick. Epizooties of some kind. She's always calling in sick, with Petie having to cover for her. He don't mind, though. I think he needs the overtime. His family's business isn't doing too well right now." The Hitzers owned Old MacDonald's Dairy, a 40-cow farm. Lately they had been getting strong competition from Sealtest, which had installed a big processing plant over near Burpyville.

"Yes, I know the Hitzers. We get our milk from them."

"They got contented milk cows."

"Back to Chief Gochnauer – you're saying he had a meeting Friday afternoon, so he clocked out early?"

"That's about the size of it. Like I told Chief Purdue this morning, I sure wish I knew who he was meeting with. It might've been his murderer."

~ ~ ~

Cookie got off the phone with J. Harold Wentworth, the ambulance chaser who had handled the Wayne estate. He told her he'd given the only key to the gate at Injun Woods to Ben Bentley, the Badger Patrol troop leader. He also confirmed that the six-foot-high barbed-wire fence surrounded the entire 40-acre parcel of land. No other way in, unless you wanted to swim under the span of fence crossing a tributary of the Wabash.

The lawyer obviously didn't know Cookie was Ben Bentley's wife, and kept trying to put suspicion onto him. "That troop leader's the only guy with a key, so if anybody let your police chief onto the property it had to be him."

"Mr. Bentley says he didn't do that."

"But can you believe him? He's a very threatening-looking guy. With all them muscles, I'd bet that ugly pug could strangle a man without even working up a sweat."

"Yes, I do believe him. And for the record, I think he's kinda cute."

"Everybody to his or her own taste," muttered the lawyer before hanging up. "The guy looks to me like he could be a stone-cold killer."

Next Cookie checked the property records at the Town Hall. Fortunately, they had been computerized last year. It didn't take her long to confirm that Injun Woods – designated as Plat No. 24674J-279 – had been in the Wayne family since the area had been settled in the early 1800s. Elmer Jackson Wayne had owned the wooded acreage since his father died in 1949.

Being a tad OCD, she also checked the marriage and birth records. Elmer had no children nor any known living relatives. A virtual recluse, he had lived in a small cottage down near Flynn's Texaco. He had no wife, no housekeeper, no yardman, no property manager.

No one to trust with a key.

So how did Evers Gochnauer get in?

Chapter Eight

Man on a Mission

Ben Bentley was indeed a short fireplug of a man, his bulging muscles making him almost as wide as tall. He'd been a high school wrestling champion forty-some years ago and still had the physique. Now a retired farmer, he'd married Cookie after her first husband got killed in a tractor accident involving a necktie caught in a John Deere engine. (A lesson against plowing while wearing your Sunday finest.)

Ben and Cookie made a great couple, high school sweethearts reunited. She was something of a faded beauty queen, her blonde hair and blue eyes hinting of an allure that lingered behind schoolmarmish spectacles and lack of makeup. As for Benjamin Bartholomew Bentley, he may have looked like a bearded troll straight out of a J. R. R. Tolkien novel, but neighbors and friends found him to be a gentle, kind-hearted man. He divided his time between Sons of Anthony Wayne and the Haney Bros. Circus and Petting Zoo. Both had a common denominator: Helping kids.

Marrying later in life, Ben and Cookie had no kids of their own. Cookie avoided the topic by burying herself in her two passions, quilt making and local history. Ben kept the petting zoo going with the help of Bombay Martinez. Big Bill Haney had retired after losing his wife Willamina to cancer last year.

Also, Ben treated the twelve members of the Badger Patrol as if they were his own. He felt protective of them. He liked taking them camping.

Around noon Ben dropped by the Dollar General to pay the manager for the Almond Joy candy bar he'd got there the other day. The man had a sweet tooth. At the time he didn't have any money on him, so the manager said to pay him later. Caruthers Corners was that kind of town, where you trusted other people.

Donald Smyth had only been manager of the Dollar General little over a year. He and his family had moved here from Terre Haute. His son Buddy was a member of the Badger Patrol.

"How's Buddy doing?" the troop leader asked. The boy had been the first to spot the dead body up at Injun Woods.

"Don't worry about Buddy. He's a resilient little guy. Nothing bothers him."

"Good to hear that."

"That camping-trip-that-didn't-happen is all he talks about. He'd never seen a dead man before."

"Well –"

"Gotta see one sooner or later. That's a part of life," said Donald Smyth. "May as well get prepared for it."

"Yeah, I see your point," nodded Ben as he forked over a $20 bill, picked up two more Almond Joys, and waited for his change. Hot Tamales were the most popular candy in Indiana, according to a recent survey. But the squat farmer was an Almond Joy kinda guy. He liked the nuts mixed with coconut and chocolate.

After pocketing his change, Ben waved the manager goodbye and made his way to the back of the store where Tommy Truehart was stocking shelves. Tommy had worked here ever since graduating high school. He was a skinny kid with shaggy hair, wearing the black polo and dark trousers that reflect the company's approved dress code. He looked up as Ben approached.

"Hi, Tommy. How's your Aunt Enid doing?" the squat man greeted the boy.

"Hello, Mr. Bentley. She's taking Evers' death pretty hard. I almost hate going home. All she does is cry and talk about selling the house."

"Why sell the house?"

"Says she can't make it without Evers' salary. Claims she's gonna move into an assisted living facility. Don't know where I'd live. I don't make that much here at Dollar General."

"If it comes to it, I've got a one-bedroom place up near Never Ending Swamp I could rent you cheap," offered Ben Bentley. "Ain't much, but it would be a roof over your head." A few years back, Tommy had been a member of the Badger Patrol. Ben took care of his boys.

"Thank you kindly, Mr. Bentley. I hope it don't come to that."

"Tommy, I don't wanna disturb you at work, but I have a quick question to ask."

"Is it about Evers?"

"Yeah, it is. I was wondering if you talked with him last Friday?"

"Sure. I saw him that afternoon. He stopped by Dollar General to tell me I'd have to get my own ride home. Said he had to go see his deputy, that Viola Whatzername."

"Did he say why?"

"Something about heading off a scandal. Some lawyer in Burpyville let it slip that she was having a fling with one of his clients."

"So what? She's single, isn't she?"

"Yeah, but the guy isn't. He's got a wife and kid, Evers said."

"Awkward."

"Evers didn't want a member of the police department getting caught up in an ugly divorce. He felt it would reflect badly on him, being new on the job and all. He took it seriously, being police chief."

~ ~ ~

Beauregard Madison stood on the steps of the Town Hall and surveyed the neat rows of Victorian homes that surrounded the Town Square. A few years ago he'd been mayor of this small municipality. That was following the scandalous reign of Henry Caruthers. Managing a town – even a small one – had been quite a handful. He didn't regret turning the job over to his son-in-law. Mark Tidemore had the makings of a fine mayor.

Beau's white hair ruffled in the breeze. He was a tall beanpole of a man. He would've been a proper subject for that Spanish Renaissance painter El Greco, the one known for his elongated figures. Quiet mannered and soft spoken, Beau was a well-liked member of the community. Born and raised here like his wife and all their friends. A true Hoosier at heart.

In the distance, he could see the big Ferris wheel churning against the wide blue sky. Kids squealed as they reached out from the gondolas pretending to grab at clouds. Maybe next year the town could afford to add a carousel.

Beau shifted his glance toward the large koi pond in the middle of the park. Just beyond the flash of splashing goldfish he could see the copse of bronze statues. Three of them represented the founders of Caruthers Corners – Jacob Caruthers, Ferdinand Jinks, and his own great-grandfather, Beauregard Madison. These brave men had led the wagon train that brought the first settlers to this rolling green countryside near the Wabash River.

The tribes of Potawatomi who resided here had not been quite as welcoming as those Wampanoag who shared that Thanksgiving dinner with the Pilgrims. However, the Battle of Gruesome Gorge had helped establish the white settlers' land claim. Following a series of treaties, the Potawatomi were forcibly relocated westward in 1838. This marked the single largest Indian removal in Indiana's history.

Beau wrote it off as a sordid page in the state's past, but his wife Maddy took the topic of Native America Rights much more seriously. If left up to her, she'd give the town back to the Potawatomi.

Despite all this, Beau and Maddy loved this small Indiana town. They were proud to call it home.

Too bad an occasional crime or misdeed put a blotch on its record. Like the murder of its police chief.

Beau had been thinking about Evers Gochnauer's mysterious death. Surely, no one in Caruthers Corners could do something terrible like this. He'd developed his own theory about who might have committed the crime. This had to be the work of "outside elements."

But who?

He decided it had to be gypsies. Or hobos.

Chapter Nine

Deputy at the DQ

As Maddy was leaving the police department, she noticed a cruiser parked two doors down at the Dairy Queen. Deputy Pete Hitzer having his usual lunch, a footlong hot dog and Cherry Coke. He survived on a limited diet of junk food.

Now would be a good time to talk with him, Maddy decided. Get him to confirm he'd been filling in for – what was her name? – Viola Fahrner. Maybe Chief Gochnauer had said something to him when he switched the schedule.

"Hi, Petie," she greeted the deputy. He was sitting at the concrete table next to the DQ take-out window. "Mind if I join you?"

"Oh, hello, Mrs. Madison. Sit down. Want a French fry?"

"No thanks. I'm just poking around, trying to figure out what happened to Evers."

"Figured you Quilters Clubbers would be asking questions. Chief Purdue won't be happy about that – but what's new?"

"He appreciates our help more than you think."

Petie Hitzer sniggered. "If Chief Purdue had any hair, he'd be pulling it out."

"Well, maybe."

"Whatcha wanna know about Evers' murder?"

"Why was he out at Injun Woods?"

"Beats me. He was supposed to be meeting with Viola – that's the other deputy – but she says he never showed up."

"Where were they meeting?"

"Her house. She was home sick. That's why I was on duty Friday night. Filling in for her."

"Anybody have a grudge against Evers?"

"Half the town. He was a pushy cop. Don't know why he got picked over me to be the new chief."

"Did you resent that?"

"Do you mean did I kill him because he got the job I wanted? No, I didn't. And Myrtle Dobbler can vouch for me. When I wasn't sitting at the station with her, I was making my rounds, staying in contact with her on the radio every hour of the night."

"Nobody's accusing you, Petie. Everybody knows you're a straight-shooter. Beau told me he voted for you to be the new chief."

"Your husband's a good guy. He was a good mayor too, not that your son-in-law isn't top drawer."

"Thanks, Petie. But we have to figure out who would have done this to Evers."

"Yeah, I know. I never particularly liked him, even in high school. He was always a bully. But we worked together as deputies for fifteen years. We got along well enough."

"You say you and Myrtle talked back and forth on the radio all night long?"

"That's right. The night shift gets kinda lonely."

"I thought she worked days."

"We switch around."

When does she get sleep?"

"Oh, Myrtle takes one 12-hour shift, her sister Elvira the other. But they mix 'em up."

"Tell me, why was Evers meeting with Deputy Fahrner?"

"He didn't say. Got a phone call Friday afternoon. Quick as he hung up he said to me, 'I gotta go see Viola.'"

"Who was that call from – Viola?"

"Dunno. He phoned in later to tell Myrtle he wouldn't be back that day."

"Maybe I should ask Viola about it myself. Can you give me her address?"

"Don't really know it. She lives somewhere up near Bottomless Sinkhole, but I've never been to her house. Ask Myrtle. She'd have it on file."

~ ~ ~

Traipsing back to the police department, some twenty steps in all, Maddy barged into building. Myrtle Dobbler looked up guiltily, having just stuffed the remaining cookies into her mouth. Not saving any for her fellow cops, the tin on her desk was empty.

"Sorry," the dispatcher said. "I couldn't help myself. Them cookies were just calling to me."

"Don't worry," said Maddy. "I'll bake some more."

"That'd be nice. They were quite tasty." She dabbed at her mouth with a paper napkin.

"I just saw Petie Hitzer. He said Chief Gochnauer got a phone call right before he left the office on Friday."

"Evers got lotsa calls. Mr. Popularity after he got that promotion to police chief."

"Try to recall the people who phoned him on Friday afternoon — it's important."

Myrtle pursed her lips to think. "Friday afternoon. I remember he got a call from the Mayor, a call from his cousin Tommy, a complaint about somebody playing music too loud, and a call about a lost cat."

"Which call was last of the day?"

She opened a log book and ran her finger down the page marked "Friday." Her finger stopped. "Oh yes, here it is, two thirty-five p.m. Right before he left. A call from J. Harold Wentworth, the lawyer who handled Elmer Jackson Wayne's estate."

"What did they talk about?"

"How would I know? The Chief took the call in his office. Petie was in there with him at the time. I was out here at the switchboard."

"Oh. Well, never mind. Can you give me Deputy Fahrner's home address?"

"Yes, ma'am. No problem, I've got it right here," Myrtle Doppler said, shuffling through a file on her desk. "Tell Viola I said to get her lazy butt back to work. We're shorthanded without her."

Chapter Ten

The Other Deputy

Viola Fahrner rented a small house up near the Bottomless Sinkhole, a 40-foot-wide opening that swallowed a two-bedroom house back in 1989. Although there had never been another sinkhole near here, rentals in the area remained dirt cheap.

Sinkholes are actually more common in southern Indiana, a characteristic of the state's karst geology – dissolvable limestone bedrock. It works like this: Acidic rainwater percolates through cracks in the bedrock, slowly dissolving the limestone and over time creating sinkholes, caves, and other features that characterize karst terrain. Sometimes a cave collapses, taking everything on top with it.

More than 300,000 sinkholes are said to pockmark the major karst areas of Indiana. However, the northeastern sector of the state remains fairly safe. But try telling that to the Brandenbergers, the family whose house sits at the bottom of the Bottomless Sinkhole.

Maddy parked her Toyota Sequoia next to the mailbox and walked up to the front door. Before she could knock, the oak 2-panel door swung open. "I recognize you," said the pretty mocha-colored woman. "You're one of them Quilters Club ladies. Madelyn Madison, that's your name."

"Yes, it is –"

"You and your hubby are good friend with Chief Purdue and his wife. I've seen you around."

"Friends since high school."

"Come right in, come right in," Viola Fahrner held the door open. "I always wanted to talk with one of you Quilter Club ladies. I do a little quilting myself."

"Thank you," said Maddy, stepping into a cozy living room. A matching charcoal gray couch and chair crowded the room. The mauve hand-loomed shag rug looked new. A multicolored patchwork quilt hung on the far wall. A Grandma Moses reproduction – a primitive barnyard scene – decorated another. The faint hint of hyacinth wafted in the air, Glade's Enchanted Floral Garden scent. "You have a lovely home, Deputy."

"Call me Viola. I'm off duty. Out sick with a migraine. I get them something fierce. Like somebody's doing brain surgery without anesthetics."

"I'm sorry to hear that."

"Chief Purdue wasn't so sympathetic. But Chief Gochnauer has been more flexible about sick leave."

"Yes, Jim Purdue can be a stickler," Maddy admitted. Her friend ran a by-the-book police department, no question about that.

"What brings you out here to the sticks?" asked Viola Fahrner, offering her visitor a seat on the doily-covered armchair.

"You *are* pretty much alone out here," Maddy observed. This remote address in the northwest corner of the county was about a mile from the sinkhole; three miles from Injun Wood. No neighbors within sight.

"Most of the surrounding land is owned by Aitkens Produce. There aren't even any Amish farms near this place. A wonder electricity runs out this far. But it's the best I can afford on a deputy's salary."

The town of Caruthers Corners had a limited budget for its public servants. Evers Gochnauer had lived with his mother; Petie Hitzer lived on the family farm. The Purdue household was nice, but modest.

"I wanted to ask you about Chief Gochnauer's last day. According to Petie Hitzer, he left work early to come see you."

Viola Fahrner ducked her head, avoiding eye contact. "Like I told Chief Purdue when he called me, Evers never showed up."

"So you knew he was coming to see you?"

There was a slight pause, as if she were choosing her words carefully. "Uh, yes. Evers phoned ahead. Around three o'clock. Said he was coming out. But I never seed him. Waited around all afternoon."

"Did he say what he wanted to see you about?"

"No, he didn't. I thought maybe he was coming to fire me."

"Why would he do that?"

"Too many sick days."

"I thought you said Evers was flexible on that."

"He was. That is, up to a point. I've gone way over my allotment. But I simply can't work when a migraine comes on."

"You seem okay now."

Viola Fahrner brushed her hair back with a hand, a nervous gesture. "It cleared up right before you got here. They come and go, you know."

Maddy noticed the quilt displayed on the wall over the couch. "Oh, is that one of your quilts?"

"Yes, my attempt to do a Charm quilt."

Charm quilts are quite a challenge to make, in that they use a different fabric for each piece of the pattern. A quilt often contains hundreds of different fabrics. That makes them very time consuming. Most Charm quilts date from the 1870s. After fading in popularity around the turn of the Century, the quilts enjoyed a brief return in the 1930s. The effort to gather hundreds and hundreds of differing scraps tends to discourage modern-day quiltmakers. Only a few Charm quilts are found today.

"That's quite an undertaking," acknowledged Maddy. "You've done a very nice job."

"Really? That's quite a compliment coming from a Quilters Clubber."

"Have you never talked about quilting with Chief Purdue's wife, Bootsie? She's a member of the Quilters Club."

"Couldn't bring myself to do that. After all, she was married to my boss."

"I'm sure she would be interested in seeing your work. The other quilting bee members too."

"I'd be flattered." Her face darkened with a blush.

"Mind if I look at your Charm quilt more closely?"

"Help yourself," said the deputy, stepping aside.

Maddy walked around the coffee table and leaned over the sagging gray couch. She examined the quilt from side-to-side, top-to-bottom. "Your stitching is excellent," she observed.

"That's a special quilt to me," blurted Viola Fahrner. "I made it to commemorate me and my boyfriend's anniversary – one full year together."

"Oh? Who is your boyfriend?" asked Maddy. "Maybe I know him."

Viola began to sputter. "Uh, w-well, you see, I-I can't –"

"Can't what?"

"– c-can't talk about him. He wants us to keep it a secret."

"Why is that?"

"Well, uh, I-I can't say."

That meant he was married, Maddy concluded. But who could it be? Then she noticed something about the quilt and had her answer.

Chapter Eleven
The Badge

At that moment Howie Oakman was sitting in the police chief's office with Jim Purdue and Doc Medford. Myrtle had made a fresh pot of coffee. The office furniture was all askew, because the acting chief and his deputy had not finished putting it back into place. What had Evers Gochnauer been thinking when he'd rearranged it? Everything had been just right the way it was. If the man hadn't been dead, Jim would have considered throttling him ... although that was unfortunate phraseology, given the man's manner of death.

Oakman slid the silver badge across the desk. "Here you go. Found it near the mound in Injun Woods."

"Hmm," said Jim Purdue, turning it over in his fingers, examining the badge. The word DEPUTY was engraved below a star-shape. "Evers must have lost it in the struggle."

"That's what I thought."

"Funny that he was wearing his Deputy's badge rather than Chief of Police," mused Jim Purdue.

Doc Medford spoke up: "He *was* wearing his Chief of Police badge. It was still pinned on his uniform. Got it in his property box over at the Mortuary. I was gonna turn it over to his mama with the rest of his belongings. A wallet, car keys, assorted change, a pack of gum. And that badge."

"You don't say?" Jim Purdue frowned. "Then where did this badge come from?"

"Beats me," shrugged Howie Oakman. "It was just lying there in the leaves. A few feet from where Gochnauer was murdered."

Doc Medford hesitated. "Hate to break the news like this ... I was gonna save it for my autopsy report. But Evers Gochnauer wasn't killed atop that pile of dirt."

That got everyone's attention. "You're saying he wasn't killed on that Indian mound where he body was found?"

"Pretty sure not. Based on the lividity."

"Lividity?" said Dr. Howard Carvel Oakman. As a paleontologist he was used to dealing with bones. Or petrified versions of them. Not fleshy corpses that contained blood.

"Postmortem lividity is the settling of blood in the lower portions of the body following death. When the heart quits pumping, the red blood cells sink through the serum by action of gravity. That produces a purplish red discoloration of the skin that's on the bottom. Livor mortis starts within about 20 minutes following death but isn't visible for about two hours."

Jim Purdue snorted. "Thanks for the lecture, Dr. Frankenstein. But what's that got to do with Evers Gochnauer?"

"When the Badger Patrol discovered Evers Gochnauer's body, he was lying belly-up. That means the regions of his back that didn't touch the ground should have been a dark purple due to the settling of blood. And it was. But here's the kicker: There were also signs of lividity on his chest. Lividity on both sides of the body indicates he had been moved after death."

"If he wasn't killed there, where?" asked Jim Purdue.

"Beats me. Aren't any houses up that way that I can think of. Just that big sinkhole and acres of scrub pines."

"Exactly when did he die?"

"Based on the temperature of his liver, I'd say he'd been dead about six hours when I examined the body. The formula is quite simple: 37.5°C - 1.5°C. That means the body loses 1.5°C per hour until its temperature matches the environment around it."

"Six hours? The Badgers found him around 8:30 a.m. Took you a half hour to get there. That means he died at 3:00 a.m."

"That sounds about right," nodded the coroner.

"That's pretty late for Evers to be out," observed Jim Purdue. "He should've been home in bed at that time of night."

"Did he have a wife?" asked Howie Oakman.

"Nope," Jim shook his head. "Lived with his mother."

"How's she taking it?" Doc Medford wanted to know. He'd been the family physician for ages. Last year he'd treated Enid Gochnauer's gall bladder. And removed Evers' appendix the year before that.

"About as badly as you'd expect. He was an only child, y'know."

"Yeah, but a cousin lived with 'em. A boy named Tommy Truehart. Enid's sister's kid. Enid took him in after her sister died from conjunctivitis."

"Pink eye?"

"It got infected. I coulda saved her if she'd been my patient. But she lived over in Burpyville. Had some quack I'd never heard of."

"Still can't figure out what Evers was doing out at Injun Woods in the middle of the night," Jim Purdue shook his head.

"Remember what Doc just said," Howie Oakman pointed out. "Your friend may have been killed somewhere else, then dumped on the mound for the Badger Patrol to find."

"Maybe the killer didn't know those kids were going to be out there the next morning," Chief Purdue adjusted the theory.

"Could be he thought Injun Woods was simply a good hiding place for a dead body," nodded Doc Medford. "If those kids hadn't shown up it might've not been found for years."

"Yeah, but one thing still bothers me. How in heck did the killer get in?" said Jim Purdue. "That place was locked up tight. And there was only one key."

Chapter Twelve

Return to Cozy Café

Four o'clock on the dot, everybody reconvened at Cozy Café. Maisie had fresh coffee ready. She delivered it to the corner booth along with slices of watermelon pie without waiting for an order. The extra chair was already in place.

"Well, what do you girls have to report?" Maddy called the meeting to order with no further ado.

Bootsie spoke first: "The coroner says Evers was strangled by an Indian."

"You mean by a Native American?" asked Maddy, always politically correct.

Bootsie nodded. "Yes, an Indian," she repeated. "Doc Medford bases that opinion on the type of rope used to strangle Evers. A kind made by Indians, judging by the fibers."

"But there aren't any Indians – Native Americans, I mean – in Caruthers Corners," said Maddy.

"Except for Matea Davis," reminded Cookie.

"Oh yes, Matea," acknowledged Maddy.

"That little Indian brave," sighed Lizzie. "He's such a cutie. Surely he doesn't qualify as a cold-blooded killer."

"Besides," observed Bootsie, "he doesn't have a motive." Her husband Jim had always said to look for Motive, Means, and Opportunity.

"Maybe Matea's getting revenge because our forefathers stole his people's land," suggested Cookie. She was always a historian at heart.

"That's pretty farfetched," said Lizzie. The idea had to be pretty far off base for Lizzie to consider it "farfetched." She was the Queen of Crazy Theories.

"Don't forget The Trail of Death," countered Cookie. In 1838 US militia had removed 859 Potawatomi from their land in Indiana and marched them to reservations in the West. On the trip 42 people died. "I'd be pretty unhappy if that happened to my great-grandparents," she said.

"Yes, but —"

Maddy raised a silencing hand. "Hold on," she said calmly. "Let's go about this in a logical fashion. The coroner said an Indian might be involved. And Matea is, in fact, a Native American. So he should be added to our list of suspects."

"Okay," Lizzie accepted the decision. "But I still think he's cute. Kind of a redskin version of Brad Pitt."

"You're right," agreed Bootsie. "Have you ever seen Matea without his shirt?"

"One time at the Community Pool," grinned Lizzie. "He was acting as lifeguard. What a handsome six-pack he has. He must exercise a lot."

"Oooo, be still my beating heart!"

"Ladies!" Maddy called them to order. Uncomfortable with that "redskin" reference. Even the football teams were under pressure to give up racially insensitive names like that. Even the Caruthers Corners Potawatomi – a local middle-school baseball team – had changed their name to the Caruthers Corners Pioneers.

"Who else should go on that list?" asked Cookie, stifling a smile.

Bootsie cleared her throat and said, "Jim said Matea accused Pete Hitzer. He said Petie was jealous that Evers got the Chief of Police job when Jim stepped down."

"Oh my goodness. Petie is as trustworthy as a Boy Scout," declared Lizzie. "He worked as a teller at the bank before he went into law enforcement." Elizabeth Kay Ridenour's grandfather had founded Caruthers Corners Savings & Loan. And for years her husband Edgar had been its president. She knew all the employees, past and present.

"Nonetheless, Petie goes on the list," decided Maddy.

"Anybody else?" asked Cookie. Keeping track.

"Did Elmer Jackson Wayne have any relatives?" inquired Lizzie. "Somebody who might have attacked Evers for trespassing?"

"Nope, not a single descendant," pronounced Cookie. Recalling the Wayne family's genealogy chart. A straight line from a distant cousin of Mad Anthony Wayne to ol' Elmer himself. No branches or offshoots.

"What about moonshiners who might've mistaken him for a revenue agent?"

"This is not Appalachia," snorted Cookie.

"You never know ..."

"I can assure you there's no moonshine still in Injun Woods," said Bootsie.

"How so?"

"No way to haul sugar in or mash out." QED – *Quod erat demonstrandum.*

"Don't forget, the gate was locked," added Cookie. "Ben said he had to use the key to get in that morning they found the body."

"And there was only one key?"

"Yes," nodded the blonde historian. "I spoke with the lawyer for the Wayne estate. He assured me he gave the only key to Ben."

"Could someone have borrowed Ben's key without him knowing and made a duplicate?"

Cookie shook her head. "Ben said the key never left his key ring. He carries them on a chain attached to his belt."

"Forget the key for a minute," said Bootsie. "I want to know what Evers was doing up there in Injun Woods. He was supposed to be off duty Friday night."

"I might be able to partially answer that," responded Maddy. "Those watermelon cookies I delivered to Myrtle Dobbler got me one interesting piece of information. The last call she took for Chief Gochnauer on Friday afternoon was from that lawyer, J. Harold Wentworth."

"What?" exclaimed Cookie. "When I spoke with him earlier today he didn't mention anything about having a conversation with Evers Gochnauer."

"Hmm, that seems suspicious," said the police chief's wife. "Maybe he's got something to hide?"

"What did he call Evers about?" asked Lizzie. All ears. She loved intrigue. "Was he luring the police chief to Injun Woods?"

"Myrtle said she didn't know."

"That's impossible," declared Bootsie. "She's the police department's dispatcher. She eavesdrops on *every* call. At least that's what Jim says."

"Well, she didn't tell me."

Lizzie said, "I'm betting Evers went to Injun Woods to meet that shady lawyer and something went wrong. They had a fight and Wentworth killed him."

Bootsie shook her head doubtfully. "No, that doesn't work. The coroner says Evers was killed somewhere else and moved to Injun Woods."

"There you have it. Viola Fahrner did it," said Lizzie. Switching theories as fast as changing a sweater. "Killed him at her house, then dumped the body. She lives up there near Injun Woods."

"Yes, but the coroner also said Evers was killed by an Indian," Maddy reminded them. "Viola looked black to me."

"She is," confirmed Bootsie. "I saw her application when Jim hired her. She listed her race as African American."

"Is she from around here?"

"No, Viola worked for the Indy PD before coming here. But she's originally from the Deep South, as I recall. A small town in Alabama called Hobson City."

"I know about Hobson City. It's an all-black town founded by freed slaves," said Cookie, drawing on her trick memory. "When it was incorporated in 1899, an Alabama newspaper described it as 'the only municipality controlled and governed entirely by colored people anywhere in the United States.' Today Hobson City is still 94 percent black."

"That settles that," said Maddy. Writing off Viola Fahrner as a suspect.

Lizzie tried another tact. "What about this lawyer? Is *he* an Indian?"

"I doubt it," Maddy shook her head. "Wentworth doesn't much sound like an Indigenous American name."

"It's not," confirmed Cookie. "The name is English in origin." Apparently, she was quite knowledgeable on the etymology of names too.

"J. Harold Wentworth – that sounds pretty WASPy to me," opined Lizzie. Being of Italian descent, she was sensitive about the social strata in a small Indiana town with a Euro-centric population. Plenty of Swiss Germans and Norwegians, not many Wops. She was mindful that W.O.P. stood for With Out Papers, a reference to many Italians' questionable immigration status. At least that was the accepted story.

"First initial with a middle name, it's an affectation," said Maddy. "You know how pompous lawyers can be." Then she caught herself: "I don't mean my son-in-law Mark, of course."

"Oh, come on. Mark is definitely a WASP," laughed Lizzie. "A White Anglo-Saxon Protestant – just like all of you!"

"Us?"

"Don't try to deny it. You're all privileged white upper middle-class ladies."

"Ha! You're an Italian WASP," retorted Bootsie.

"What's that?"

"An affluent guido who takes great pride in her appearance and likes to shop at Ann Taylor."

"Touché!" said Lizzie. She was a shopaholic. She practically supported Lord & Taylor, Lands' End, Talbots, and Ann Taylor.

"Wentworth," continued Cookie. Showing off that super memory. "It's what linguists call a habitational name, one that describes where a person's ancestors came from. For instance, there's a civil parish in South Yorkshire – that's in England – called Wentworth. The name probably has the same root as Winterbottom or Wynterwade."

Maddy rolled her eyes. It sometimes drove her crazy that her friend was a walking encyclopedia.

Bootsie sniggered. Enjoying the byplay.

Not to be sidetracked, Lizzie reframed her question. "What else do we know about this lawyer?"

"Not much," Maddy admitted. "Just that he was the attorney of record for Elmer Jackson Wayne. That he turned the key to Injun Woods over to Ben. And that he telephoned Chief Gochnauer on Friday afternoon. As far as we know, he's the last person to talk with Evers before he died."

"That doesn't tell us much," grumbled the banker's wife.

"Sorry, but I don't have a family tree in my files for any Wentworths," said Cookie. "He must not be from around here."

Bootsie snorted. "Ha! You're wrong about that. Johnny Wentworth's actually a local guy. He attended Caruthers High a few years behind us."

"You're sure?" Maddy raised her eyebrows. That look of surprise that Ellen Burstyn had given Nicolas Cage in *The Wicker Man.*

"My cousin dated him," Bootsie nodded. "She said he was a sharp dresser, but otherwise a complete dolt. Barely graduated high school. She can't believe he actually got a law degree."

"How come I've never heard of a Wentworth family hereabouts?" puzzled the blonde historian.

"Because Johnny was a transfer student. He came here to live with his grandparents. His mother was a Yager."

"Oh," said Cookie. Relieved that the gap in her knowledge was legitimate. "I know the Yager family. Hank and Emily live over on Melon Seed Road. Their boy Georgie is in Ben's Beaver Patrol. A timid little fellow."

"Well, his dad's certainly not timid," said Lizzie. "Hank Yager's a big blustery yahoo. I hear he's quite a tyrant at home."

"That's true," confirmed the police chief's wife. "Jim says there've been quite a few domestic disturbance complains at the Yager household."

"That doesn't surprise me," said Lizzie. "The man's definitely got a violent streak."

"How well do you know Hank Yager?" asked Cookie. Surprised at her friend's strong reaction.

"Me? Not well, but Edgar does. Had to kick him out of the bank for starting a row with a teller a few years ago. Claimed that he didn't get the right change."

"What happened?"

"Edgar gave him the dime in dispute out of his own pocket. Even so, Yager closed his account. He's a surly, hot-tempered jerk, you ask me."

"But he's not an Indian – a Native American, that is," Maddy pointed out.

"Actually, Yager is of German-Dutch origin," Cookie informed them. "An occupational surname meaning 'hunter.'"

"I wonder if Doc Medford might be on the wrong track with all this Indian business," said Maddy. "Last month the Badger Patrol was learning how to make rope from various vines and plants. Part of their woodlore program. N'yen was busy gathering all kinds of vines and drying them out to make rope. It was a big project for the boys."

"Your point?"

"That lots of people could have made the rope that strangled Evers."

"There are only a dozen or so kids in the Badger Patrol," said Bootsie. "It wouldn't be hard to check out each of their families. See if we turn up anyone suspicious."

Cookie heaved a sigh. "Are you proposing we put Ben and the families of his entire troop on our list of suspects?" she said. Not bothering to hide the exasperation in her voice.

"No, of course not," replied Bootsie. Quickly backing off her suggestion. "No one thinks the Sons of Anthony Wayne are behind Evers' murder."

"The Badger Patrol – they're just little kids," said Lizzie.

"Except for Ben," fumed Cookie. "That lawyer practically accused him, saying he was the only person with a key."

"Look," said Maddy. "Let's make it a rule that husbands are above suspicion."

"I second that," said Bootsie.

"Easy for you to say," laughed Cookie. Breaking the tension. "*Your* hubby is the chief of police.

"And mine was a bank president," added Lizzie. "Despite having the combination to the vault, he hardly embezzled a penny."

"I'm not so sure about that," teased Bootsie. "You do have a pretty nice house."

"Ha!" replied the redhead. "The house was paid for with my family money. But come to think of it, my grandfather likely stole most of it before coming over from Italy."

"Well, that's decided," said Cookie. Obviously relieved. "Our husbands are off the table when it comes to suspects."

"Yes. But I do think we should look more closely at J. Harold Wentworth," suggested Maddy. "There's something about him that's just not right."

~ ~ ~

After that, Bootsie had to go home and walk her dogs. Inka, Dinka, and Doo had a fenced-in backyard, but they enjoyed long off-the-leash runs on the rolling pastures of Old MacDonald's Dairy. The Purdues lived in a modest house adjacent to the big farm. The dogs ignored the cows, preferring to sniff out rabbits and squirrels. The Hitzer family didn't mind Bootsie and her dogs roaming the "back forty" in that Jim Purdue was their son's boss.

Cookie popped back over to the museum to check on her docents. They were volunteers, requiring oversight and supervision. Cookie's assistant did a good job of that, but sometimes she needed a little supervision herself.

Lizzie had an appointment to get her nails done at Helen of Troy Spa and Beauty Salon. She was going to try a new shade of red – Ruby Tuesday, it was called. If she had time, she'd get a pedicure too. She liked looking her best.

Maddy always tried to be home when N'yen and Aggie got off from school. She usually had cookies and milk waiting on the kitchen table. But lately Aggie had been lingering more often after class with Bobby Elwood. And N'yen was starting to hang out in the Town Square. The Ferris wheel and a nearby ice cream truck had turned the park into a popular gathering place for local kids. After all, Caruthers Corners didn't have a mall.

Chapter Thirteen
She No Longer Waited

Aggie was late getting home. First thing she did was feed her dog. That had been the deal when she got Tige – she would be responsible for taking care of him.

"Where's N'yen," asked her mother. Aggie's cousin was usually trailing along behind her.

"At the park. But he'll be along shortly. Grammy promised us watermelon cookies today. She baked up a batch for the folks at the police station."

"Feeding the poor?"

"More like bribing a police officer," she giggled.

"What?"

"Don't hold dinner. N'yen and I will eat with Grammy and Grampy."

"Okay, dear." Tilly knew the boy's parents would be arriving tomorrow. So a "Last Supper" with his grandparents was in order. He had been part of their household for over a year now. As for Aggie, she sometimes wondered if her daughter lived here or there. The kids had been inseparable, until recently.

Tilly Tidemore hoped she and Mark were doing the right thing, letting Aggie start "dating" at fifteen. Bobby Elwood was a nice boy and the dates were harmless outings to the movies or group activities. Safe enough.

N'yen made a good chaperon, but Aggie shunned her cousin when going to the AMC Multiplex in Burpyville. Fortunately, these were double-dates with Pricilla Moretz and her boyfriend Teddy DiMacchio. Of the four, Teddy D was the only one with a valid driver's license.

A sometimes outcast, N'yen had taken to hanging out in the Town Square. Lots of kids congregated there, riding the Ferris wheel, buying ice cream treats from the Mr. Ding Dong wagon, or simply carousing.

Being an English major, Tilly was reminded of a little-known poem by Tennessee Williams, a memory he wrote of his sister Rose. Young Tom had felt betrayed when Rose entered into puberty and began to be interested in other boys.

> *"At fifteen my sister no longer waited for me, impatiently at the White Star Pharmacy corner but plunged headlong into the discovery, Love!"*

These words reminded her of N'yen, lingering at the bandstand in the Town Square, waiting for the cousin on whom he doted. But she was off holding hands with Bobby Elwood.

~ ~ ~

Lizzie dropped by the Dollar General to pick up this week's copy of *National Chatterbox*. It was her favorite magazine. The manager saved her a copy under the counter, in case that week's allotment sold out. She was as regular as clockwork, stopping by to pick up the tabloid magazine.

"Thanks, Donald," she said to the manager as he handed over the prize. "Who's doing what to whom this week?"

"According to the cover, Oprah's having an affair with Morgan Freeman. And Harrison Ford's dying from King Tut's Curse, which he contracted filming that first *Indiana Jones* movie."

"Oh, look. There's a squib down here at the bottom that say Robert Downey Jr. is confined to an iron lung between *Iron Man* movies. How terrible!" Lizzie took every unsubstantiated story in the rag as gospel.

"That's a very pretty shade of lipstick you're wearing today," said the manager.

"Why thank you. It's called Ruby Tuesday."

"Like the Beatles song."

"Yes, I suppose it is. But I think it matches my hair, don't you?"

"I've always had a thing for redheads," said the manager, leaning across the counter on his elbows.

"I'll take that as a compliment," said Lizzie. She'd always found Donald Smyth a little *too* friendly. But she was a big girl, able to handle herself with mashers and flirts. Although Donald came on strong, he was harmless, she told herself.

~ ~ ~

Late that afternoon Matea Davis was working on the wooden structure next to the river, a traditional Potawatomi wigwam. The recent storm had torn away the mat that formed one of its sides. This wasn't difficult to repair, but it was time-consuming to weave a replacement mat.

His Potawatomi forbearers used cattail leaves to construct these mats, sewing them together to make a waterproof covering for a wigwam or medicine lodge.

Following tradition, Matea stitched the pieces with a bone needle (*shabneken*) and native string (*sebapIs*). He did it so carefully that the stitches were nearly invisible. Then he wrapped the edges tightly with fiber to prevent them from unravelling.

The finished mat measured five feet wide by about the same length. He fitted it over the open hole in the wigwam's side and anchored it with a strong binding to the wooden framework.

There! As good as when he'd first built the wigwam, hidden here in this primeval forest where no one would discover it.

In his language the cattail was called *pukyuk*. And the ripened fruit at the head of the cattail was known as *biwie'skwinuk*, meaning "fruit for the baby's bed." This fluffy pappus-like material was often used to create quilts for infants. Sometimes these quilts were combined with rope to make swing hammock cradles for babies. But being single, Matea had no use for baby beds or cradles, so he discarded the leftover *biwie'skwinuk*.

He wanted to fix up his wigwam for the possibility of having a visitor. He would like to share his heritage with deserving friends. That was one of the reasons he had been conducting woodlore classes for the Badger Patrol. He didn't want Potawatomi skills to be lost to history.

With his wigwam repaired, he stopped to build a fire in a rocked-walled pit. For dinner he would fry up some fish (*gigos*) in a cast-iron pan. That together with some wild rice (*pkocnomin*) and squash (*winbati*) would make a meal fit for a tribal chief.

Chapter Fourteen

Professional Courtesy

The Quilters Club got an early start the next morning. Even local farmers were barely up. Today the girls were determined to find out more about the last person known to talk with Evers Gochnauer.

"Early bird gets the worm," Maddy told herself as she made a beeline for the Town Hall. She knew her son-in-law arrived at work well ahead of other employees. He called this his "quiet time," an hour or two to get work done without interruption.

You can imagine his inward groan when Maddy appeared at his office door.

"Come on in," he waved his mother-in-law toward an empty chair. "What are you doing here at this hour?"

"I brought you some coffee," she said brightly. Plunking a paper cup on the corner of his desk. Steam curled out of it like a smoke signal. A last-second side trip, she'd caught Maisie just as she was opening Cozy Café for the breakfast crowd.

"Now I know you want something. As the saying goes, Beware of Greeks bearing gifts."

"I'm not Greek," she smiled. "But I do need a favor."

"And if I say no?"

"Then you don't get this coffee."

"Okay, okay." The mayor reached for the morning joe. Everybody knew he had a big caffeine habit. "Just tell me what you want."

Stitch in the Ditch

That's how Mark Tidemore got drafted into checking out J. Harold Wentworth's credentials. He was reluctant to do so (professional courtesy, like that joke about the sharks who wouldn't attack a lawyer), but there was no saying "no" to Maddy Madison. Not if he wanted to remain married to her daughter.

Precisely at 9 a.m. when the Indiana State Bar Association opened for business, Mark the Shark called a high-placed friend and asked him for some "off the record" info about J. Harold Wentworth. His friend (who would deny they'd ever had the conversation) mentioned Wentworth's several official censures – plus a rumor that he played fast and loose with his escrow accounts.

That was followed up with a quick call to a lawyer in Burpyville who had taken over several of Mark's accounts when he became mayor. The guy owed him big, all that ready-made billing handed to him on a silver platter. After some small talk, Mark got to the point: Turns out, the word on Wentworth was not pretty. His fellow litigators considered him toxic. He was known for his insurance cases, many of which were just short of scams.

"Stay away from him," the Burpyville lawyer concluded. "Else you may smell a strong stench."

~ ~ ~

Not letting it go at that, Lizzie called on her husband to do his part. What about those rumored escrow account violations? she politely asked in a way that left him little choice but to look into the matter ... or sleep on the couch.

As a retired bank president, Edgar Ridenour had connections. He still served on several boards. It only took a few well-placed phone calls to confirm that things were hinky with Wentworth's escrow accounts. Edgar's counterpart at Burpyville Federal let it slip that the iffy lawyer was being investigated for fraud and embezzlement. Serious charges.

The Elmer Jackson Wayne estate was one of those under scrutiny.

~ ~ ~

No, Jim Purdue didn't escape coercion from his wife either. Bootsie insisted that he check with the Feds about that rumored investigation. Rolling his eyes, the chief put in a call to his friend Neil Wannamaker, Special Agent in Charge at the Indianapolis regional office of the Federal Bureau of Investigation.

"Are you calling me because of a case you're on, or because your wife and her wannabe detectives put you up to it?" asked the FBI agent known as Neil the Nailer.

Doggone, thought Jim Purdue, that Wannamaker was pretty smart for a government employee. Nonetheless, he deflected the question with a laugh, saying, "You're a very funny fellow."

"Can't tell you much. Not my case. And I doubt you have an official need to know. But I'd predict Johnny Wentworth has a promising future as a jailhouse lawyer. With himself as his first client."

"Thanks, Neil. We'll leave it at that."

Chapter Fifteen

The Shady Lawyer

John Harold Wentworth held a law degree from Thomas M. Cooley Law School, the same institution that had graduated Michael Cohen, the scandal-ridden personal lawyer of President Donald Trump. The school had been ranked as the "worst law school in the country" by Above the Law website. And Johnny finished at the very bottom of his class.

Wentworth had handled the estate of Elmer Jackson Wayne. As Wayne's lawyer, he'd been raiding the old man's assets for years. At 87, Elmer was *non compos mentis* by any measure of the term. Had been for ages, but being a recluse nobody noticed. It was a shame when the old geezer got stung to death by his bees. Otherwise, the lawyer could have continued to "milk this cash cow" for a very long time to come.

When ol' Elmer died, Johnny Wentworth made the most of an unfortunate situation, transferring property to shell companies he controlled, closing out bank accounts, cashing in stocks. It was easy to do, in that Elmer Jackson Wayne had no living relatives.

No big deal that he'd honored Elmer's request to leave a tract of land called Injun Woods to the Sons of Anthony Wayne. Through some kind of convoluted genealogical reasoning, Elmer had been convinced he was related to "Mad Anthony." The land was worthless, a primeval forest filled with snakes and 'possums and bobcats. Let those snotty little campers have it,

Wentworth told himself. A good distraction, causing people to not question what was happening with the rest of the old man's estate.

On instructions from the SAW headquarters in Indianapolis, he had turned over the Injun Woods gate key to Ben Bentley, the local troop leader. There was one other key, but a couple of years ago he had loaned it to one of his clients, a hunter who treated the fenced-off woods as his private game preserve. Goodness knows what he found to shoot out there. Wild turkeys, maybe. Certainly not deer or other large game.

When that police chief's body had been found at Injun Woods, he got a call from some lawman by the name of Jim Purdue, asking who had access to the property. Nobody, he'd lied. Just old Elmer, he had the only key. The same one he'd turned over to that SAW troop leader. That was his story and he'd stick to it. No need to make trouble for his other client. After all, the guy was his cousin.

~ ~ ~

Beau Madison was taking the 101 Bypass, on his way to Home Depot, when he spotted a hitchhiker. The man stood on the shoulder of the road, thumb-up, waving a sign that said GOING TO INDY?

No, Beau wasn't going to Indy, but he had the impulse to stop, that "good neighbor" impulse that raged through his veins like a Midwestern virus. Back in college, and during his military service, he'd thought nothing of hitching his way around the country. But times had changed and a hitchhiker took on the overtones of a serial killer waiting to slash your throat and steal your car. When had America become so untrusting?

He considered his theory that a hobo or other outsider had killed Evers Gochnauer. Could this hitchhiker on the side of the road be the very culprit who did it?

Beau didn't buy Doc Medford's assumption that an Indian did it, just because he'd found traces of some weed used in rope making on the victim's neck. During a struggle, the killer might have grabbed a vine to strangle Evers with. After all, there were all kind of vines and such up there in Injun Woods.

As for the victim having been killed somewhere else, the lividity marks didn't prove that. He might have been murdered on that very spot where he lay, then the body flipped over on its back as the hobo searched his pockets for money.

He'd have to try out these ideas on his little buddy N'yen. That kid was smart as a whip. He'd be able to spot any holes in this hypothesis.

That's what he told himself as he drove past the hitchhiker without slowing down.

~ ~ ~

Ben Bentley felt responsible for his troop finding a dead man. Who knew what kind of trauma that might cause in impressionable twelve- and thirteen-year-old psyches? The Sons of Anthony Wayne headquarters in Indianapolis was sending out a psychologist to counsel the boys, make sure there was no lasting emotional damage to the campers.

Or lawsuits. People were so litigious these days.

The shrink wasn't coming till Friday. N'yen Madison would be back in Chicago by then, so he wouldn't get any of the counseling. But Ben wasn't too worried about N'yen. The boy had a good head on his shoulders, "smarter than the average bear," as that television cartoon used to say. And the Madisons – his closest friends – weren't likely to sue. He was more worried about the parents of that whiny little twerp, Georgie Yager.

Georgie's mom was overprotective, always smothering the kid with too much motherly love. She didn't give the boy any breathing room. He clocked up more sick days than any kid at Caruthers Corners Elementary. Georgie would need counseling for sure. Emily Yager was already complaining that her son was having nightmares about his encounter with the dead policeman.

Georgie's dad was a foreman at Aitkens Produce. Hank Yager oversaw the watermelon harvesting crews with the zealousness of an antebellum slave owner. Folks said he ran his household with the same heavy-handed approach. Emily Yager feared her husband's displeasure. Georgie was cowered in his father's presence.

Yes, Hank Yager was likely to sue. Word had it, he'd already consulted a lawyer over in Burpyville.

Ben Bentley had alerted SAW headquarters of this possibility. The organization's attorneys were standing by to deal with a frivolous lawsuit. Yager's name produced multiple hits in the Nexus Lexus database known as the Comprehensive Loss Underwriting Exchange. It showed he'd pursued two "whiplash" claims against his auto insurer, won a wrongful eviction lawsuit against a former landlord, and settled a slip-and-fall claim outside of court. There might have been others, but the CLUE report only goes back seven years.

Ben wondered if Evers Gochnauer's mother also had grounds for a lawsuit? Probably not. The property was well posted with NO TRESSPASSING signs. He had no right to be there. Even cops couldn't walk onto private property without cause.

The puzzling part was how the policeman got onto the Injun Woods property. The gate had been locked when the Badger Patrol arrived. The barbed-wire fence was quite high, difficult to climb over. And that lawyer said he'd given Ben the only key.

Another odd detail: Gochnauer's police cruiser wasn't parked anywhere near Injun Woods. It had been found parked behind the Town Hall, a distance of twenty-five miles – much too far to walk. Had he parked it there and rode up to Injun Woods with somebody else? Or had his killer dumped the car back in town to throw the cops off his tracks?

A thorough dusting of Gochnauer's cruiser turned up no fingerprints – not even his. That argued that the car had been dumped and wiped clean.

Ben Bentley didn't consider himself a detective. But he couldn't help but think about the murder. Not an everyday occurrence in peaceable little Caruthers Corners. Nonetheless, he had confidence that the Quilters Club would answer these questions. His wife had told him they were looking into the murder. Those gals were like bloodhounds when it came to solving crimes.

Police Chief Jim Purdue was one of Ben's best friends. But he'd put his money on the Quilters Club any day of the week!

Chapter Sixteen

N'yen Meets a Friend

Aggie and N'yen had walked to school together, but she left him on his own that Thursday afternoon. Bobby Elwood had invited Aggie to go over to the DQ for a mint Blizzard. Her cousin wasn't included.

That was kinda rotten, N'yen thought, this being his last day and all. He dreaded transferring schools again. Not so much the schoolwork; he could ace that. But he hated making new acquaintances. He'd been promoted past his old classmates in Chicago. He wouldn't know anybody when he went back to class.

He wandered along Main Street, crossing over into the Town Square. The 10-acre expanse of grass sprawled across the street from the boxy red-brick edifice of the Town Hall. It featured a Gothic Revival bandstand, well-stocked koi pond, a working 16-gondola Ferris wheel, and assorted bronze statues. Concerts were held there at the bandstand on Sunday nights. He would miss them. He and Aggie used to listen to the live music – usually Paul Whittaker and His Hoosier Hotshots – while sitting in the swing on her gingerbread-laden porch. She lived with her mom and dad and three little sisters in the old Taylor mansion, that blue Victorian structure facing the west side of the Square.

As N'yen crossed the park, he took in the sights and sounds. The Ferris wheel was turning like an upended carousel, afterschool kids lining up with dimes in hand.

Stitch in the Ditch

Some neighbors complained about the blaring calliope music, audible for many blocks. When the wind was just right, you could hear it all way over at Grammy and Grampy's house on Melon Pickers Row.

"Hey, N'yen!"

He heard his name being called. Turning, he was surprised to see his friend. "What are you doing here?" he asked.

"Waiting for you."

"Oh, cool."

"Wanna go have an adventure?"

"Sure," said the boy.

Chapter Seventeen
No Motive, No Means, No Opportunity

The sky was taking on a pinkish glow, promise of the approaching sunset. The Quilters Club had collected a lot of information about that crooked lawyer today. A bad actor, to be sure. But no proof that he'd killed Evers Gochnauer.

Other than one telephone conversation, there was nothing to link him to the dead police chief. Nothing to tie him to Indian rope. No way for him to get inside the gate at Injun Woods because he'd already turned the key over to Ben Bentley. As Bootsie said, No Motive, no Means, no Opportunity.

"We're getting off track," declared Maddy. "Tomorrow we'll focus on Matea Davis. He and Petie are the only two names we have left on our list of suspects."

"I don't mind checking out that cute little Indian boy," smiled Lizzie. Her red lips like a curving slice of watermelon. "Maybe he'll take his shirt off for me. I like that smooth brown skin."

"Lizzie, behave yourself," admonished Cookie. The Methodist Puritanism coming out.

"Oh, I'm just kidding. Truth is, I think investigating Matea Davis will be a big waste of time."

"Why's that?"

"Because he can't be our murderer. There's not a mean bone in his body."

"Would you girls rather we take a closer look at Petie Hitzer?" asked Maddy.

"We might be wasting our time there too," said Bootsie. "Jim vouches for him. That boy's a police deputy, for gosh sakes. One of the good guys."

"Does being a deputy make one above suspicion?" challenged Cookie. Looking quite exasperated.

"Not necessarily," said Maddy. "I certainly think we should take a look at the other deputy, Viola Fahrner. Something's going on with her."

"What do you know?" asked Lizzie. Eager for dirt.

"I think she's having an affair with a married man. She was very evasive when I questioned her. She might be lying about Evers not showing up at her place."

"Are you saying she was having an affair with Evers?" probed Lizzie.

"No, someone else." Maddy was deliberately vague. She didn't want to ruin any reputations. Gossip could spread like wildfire in a small town. Especially if Lizzie was "in the know."

"Do we have any other suspects?" asked Cookie wearily. She was getting behind in her work at the Historical Society. Her Madison Meteorite exhibit was drawing acclaim from all corners of the state after she'd loaned it to the Indiana Historical Society. She needed to spend some time coordinating the publicity.

"None other on the list," said Lizzie, checking her notes. But Cookie would have known that with her infallible memory.

"All right then," declared Maddy, "tomorrow we focus on Viola Fahrner. But right now we have to get busy. Bill and Kathy are coming for N'yen tonight. We have to pull the house together, whip up some food, and throw that little rascal a surprise going-away party he'll never forget."

~ ~ ~

Nathan "Buddy" Smyth had been telling everybody at school about discovering the dead body at Injun Woods. Buddy was the gabby sort. His chums called him "Motor Mouth."

Buddy's dad managed the Dollar General. Donald Smyth was a good-looking fellow, other than a crooked nose from playing football in high school. Those kids in Terre Haute took their sports seriously. Injuries had been considered a badge of honor.

Some said Donald Smyth was a little too flirty with his female customers, but many middle-aged women appreciated the flattery. It was something they didn't get too much of at home. Familiarity does that over time.

Smyth's wife Patricia was a ditzy woman, either unaware or unconcerned about her husband's over-friendly nature with other women. She belonged to a local macramé group that met weekly at the Hoosier State Recreational Facility. The Smyth house looked like a Jungle Gym, the walls filled with rope and twine creations. Even the bathroom was like a spiderweb of macramé art.

Buddy Smyth insisted to his classmates that he'd actually touched the dead man, but the members of the Badger Patrol knew that wasn't true. Troop leader Ben Bentley had hustled them all out of there once the body had been spotted atop the Indian mound.

Buddy was such a liar, N'yen thought.

Stitch in the Ditch

N'yen and the Smyth boy had been in the same class until the young Asian had been promoted two classes ahead. Normally, the Caruthers Corners school system frowned on kids jumping grades, but they were at a loss for what else to do with N'yen Madison. While other students his age were struggling with simple algebraic formulas, N'yen was doing quantum physics calculations in his head.

N'yen was excited to have met up with his friend there in the Town Square after school. This friend was old enough to drive, although his rattletrap old Chevy was on its last sparkplug. But it would get them to the river where their journey would begin.

Chapter Eighteen

Where's N'yen?

Aggie had been sharing a Blizzard with Bobby Elwood at the DQ when she saw her cousin shuffling up the street toward home. He looked pretty morose. She felt bad at abandoning him to get home on his own, especially on his last day before returning to Chicago ... but she wasn't going to turn down a chance to hang out with Bobby. Her first boyfriend, she had developed a big makes-your-heart-go-pitter-pat crush on him.

She was keeping track of the time, making sure she'd get back for N'yen's going-away party. All the members of the Quilters Club and their husbands would be there. As well as her dad and mom and pesky sisters. And Uncle Freddie and his family too.

Aggie's Grammy and Grampy had three grown children: Her mom, Tilly. Uncle Freddie. And N'yen's dad, Uncle Bill.

With a houseful of children, Tilly was a stay-at-home mom. Aggie's dad was the town's mayor. Everybody said he was a great mayor, bring new businesses to Caruthers Corners. The population was slowly climbing. A bigger tax base, her dad said.

Despite his disfigurement from an apartment fire, Uncle Freddie served as the town's fire chief. He and Aunt Amanda had adopted little Donna Ann a few years back. Uncle Freddie looked like the Phantom of the Opera without a mask. But he was fearless. There was no blaze he wouldn't tackle, hose and ax in hand.

Uncle Bill and Aunt Kathy were a different story. Two do-gooders determined to save the world, they had run a Youth Center in Chi-Town before they got divorced. A double-barreled midlife crisis, apparently. Everybody was pleased that they were getting back together. Well, kinda.

Aggie Tidemore was going to miss her cousin N'yen. The Vietnamese boy was her very best-est friend. His going back to Chicago made her feel sad. The other night she found herself crying over his departure. Caruthers Corners was going to be lonely without her brainiac sidekick.

Maybe she should have let her cousin join them for a mint Blizzard. It wasn't like a real date with Bobby. Just hanging out.

From the DQ, she watched as N'yen crossed the grassy expanse of the Town Square. He stopped to speak with someone, but she couldn't tell who from this distance. The guy talking to N'yen must have been a grownup, being that he was a lot taller than the small boy. She could see them walking toward the neon-covered Ferris wheel, churning slowly against the sky like a windmill. Were they going for a ride? She doubted that. No one knew it but her: N'yen was afraid of heights.

"Want another Blizzard?" said Bobby.

"Sure," she said. An excuse to be with Bobby a little longer. She wasn't late for N'yen's party. He wasn't there yet himself.

~ ~ ~

Maddy and her friends were busily preparing for N'yen's party. Bootsie and Lizzie were cleaning the house, not that the redhead was much help. Afraid she'd chip a nail. Maddy and Cookie were preparing the munchies, dips and chips and N'yen's favorite watermelon upside down cake. Beau and Edgar would be manning the big propane charcoal grill, burning the hot dogs and hamburgers to order. Meanwhile, Ben was icing bottles of soda pop – local favorites like Triple XXX root beer and Big Red – in a galvanized wash tub.

Jim got a pass, being he was working the murder case. Everyone knew any progress he made would be fed to the Quilters Club by Bootsie. He was never good at keeping secrets from his wife.

Tilly had promised to bring egg salad. Freddie's wife was down for coleslaw. Maisie – now considered part of the family – was bringing over watermelon ice cream to go with the cake. It was shaping up to be a great party. Other than the sadness of the occasion.

Aggie came in at the last minute, having just left Bobby Elwood. She'd had two mint Blizzards, effectively killing her appetite. She would have to fake it with the watermelon cake.

"Where's N'yen?" asked Maddy. "We have to get him cleaned up before his parents arrive."

"Beats me," shrugged Aggie.

"I thought he was with you."

"No, I was with Bobby. Last time I saw N'yen he was getting ready to ride the Ferris wheel with some friend of his."

"Who? I'll call his friend's house and ask them to send him right home," said Maddy. She was used to having to trace the little rapscallion down like a Most Wanted fugitive.

"Dunno. Some older guy. I didn't recognize him at a distance." Aggie was heading up the stairs for a quick shower. She'd decided to wear her blue jumper over a white blouse tonight. She wanted to make a nice impression on her Uncle Bill and Aunt Kathy. She hadn't seen them in ages.

"Wait," called Maddy. "You have to help me find your cousin. It won't be much of a party without him."

"Aw, Grammy, I'm not his babysitter."

"Aggie," came her father's stern voice. "Go look for your cousin. We don't want him to miss his own party." Mark Tidemore and Freddie Madison were in the process of hanging a banner that said HAPPY FAMILY REUNION.

"All right," she gave in. Dragging her feet as she reluctantly descended the staircase.

"I hear a car," said Lizzie. "I'll bet it's Bill and Kathy. They must have made good time from Chicago."

"Are you sure it's them?" asked Maddy, hurrying toward the front door.

"A Subaru," said Bootsie, peeking out the window. "That's what Bill drives, isn't it?"

"Oh my. Is everything ready?" Maddy looked around the living room. It appeared to be in proper order.

"Everything's fine," said her husband as he came into the room, wiping his hands on a chef's apron that

Marjory Sorrell Rockwell

said WHAT'S COOKING, GOOD LOOKING? "Open the door and let them in, hon."

"But N'yen's not home yet."

"He'll be along in a minute," Beau reassured his wife. "Now invite our son and his new/old wife inside."

"Very well," sighed Maddy, grasping the brass doorknob. She'd polished it just this afternoon and it shone like King Solomon's Treasure. "But don't make any of those new/old remarks, please."

As she opened the door, she caught Bill picking up a large cardboard envelope from the front step. "Found this," he said, handing it to his mother.

"Probably somebody left a going-away gift for N'yen," said Maddy, accepting what looked to be a FedEx package.

"Where is N'yen?" said Kathy. "I can't wait to see him. It's been almost a year."

"He'll be here shortly," Maddy offered a weak smile, pulling on the zip-tab to open the package. "He's always running late."

"That sounds like him," smiled Kathy, a little nervous to be around her husband's relatives. "Always late."

Maddy extracted a note from inside the package and read it. Her face turned as pale as her starched white blouse. "Or maybe not," she said, voice cracking.

"What's wrong?" asked Bill.

His father took the note out of Maddy's hand. He read the message and lost a little color himself. He turned to Bootsie. "You better call your husband," Beau said in almost a whisper. "N'yen's been kidnapped."

Part II

"My friend, I am old but I shall never die. I shall always live in my children, and children's children."
- New Corn, Potawatomi chief, 1795

Chapter Nineteen

The Kidnapping

Police Chief Jim Purdue examined the message, no more than a couple of sentences printed in simple block letters with a lead pencil. It read:

> I HAVE THE BOY. HE WILL BE SAFER WITH
> ME. I AM HIS PROTECTOR.

Jim Purdue frowned. "This is not good," he said with his usual sense of understatement.

"How could this happen?" cried Kathy Madison. Things like this happened in Chicago, not in a peaceful little town like Caruthers Corners. Chicago had gangs and gangsters, while her husband's hometown was as bucolic as *The Andy Griffith Show*. Kids didn't get kidnapped here!

"Don't worry, we'll get him back," said Bill in a weak attempt to reassure his wife.

"We'd better call the FBI," said Beau Madison. His hands shaking as he steadied himself against a wall. A tall beanpole of a man, at 60 he didn't offer the stoic façade he'd once had as a combat soldier in Vietnam. Maddy was afraid her husband was about to have a heart attack.

"Too soon for the FBI to come in," said Lizzie. "Don't you have to wait 24 hours?"

"No, that's a misconception," replied Aggie's dad. Mark the Shark knew about such legal details. "The FBI can get involved in the kidnapping of a child right away.

They have a special Child Abduction Response Deployment team. The 60 or so agents who make up the CARD team are deployed at the request of an FBI field office."

"I'll call the Feebies right away," declared Jim Purdue. "Neil the Nailer owes me a few favors." Neil Wannamaker was in Charge at the Indianapolis FBI office.

"When did anyone last see N'yen?" asked Freddie.

"Aggie saw him in the Town Square after school," offered Maddy. Her mind was abuzz. Who would have kidnapped her grandson? Someone seeking revenge for one of the Quilters Club cases? Several people were serving prison sentences, thanks to their work as amateur detectives. They had made enemies, no doubt.

"That's right," confirmed Aggie. "I saw him near the Ferris wheel with some older guy."

"Older guy?" said the Chief, perking up at the clue.

"Well, I think he was older. He was a lot taller than N'yen."

"Not a classmate?" Tilly asked her daughter.

"I can't be sure," admitted Aggie. "Everybody's taller than N'yen." Having skipped a couple of grades, her cousin was the smallest kid in their class. A shrimp, as she playfully called him.

"Can you describe the guy?" pressed Jim Purdue.

"Sorry. They were too far away."

"I knew we should have gotten you prescription glasses," said Aggie's mother. The girl's sight had measured 20/30 last time the school nurse checked it. Not bad, but not perfect.

"Now, sweetie, her eyes are fine," soothed Mark the Shark. "Let's keep calm till we figure out what's happening here."

"Are you sure it was N'yen you saw?" persisted her mother.

"Yes," said Aggie. "He was a long way off, but I recognized his red backpack."

"Maybe we should organize a search party," Ben Bentley spoke up. "I could call out the Beaver Patrol to help us look for N'yen."

"No, don't put all those other kids at risk," cautioned his wife Cookie. "We have a kidnapper running loose."

"I'll call out all my guys," volunteered Freddie. As Fire Chief, he had a dozen firemen and volunteers immediately available. Not to mention his paramedics crew.

"I'll have Myrtle pull in all the part-time deputies," nodded the Police Chief. "We'll cut off the roads leaving town." He reached for the kitchen wall phone as he spoke.

Freddie was already on his iPhone, talking with the fire department. Within seconds the familiar moan of the station's fire alarm filled the air. "We're going to conduct a block-by-block search," he announced as he got off his phone. "I'm going down to meet the men at the fire house, get them organized. We'll cover this town door by door."

"I'll get my troop's dads to help them put up posters," Ben revised his plan. "That should be safe."

"My poor little boy," blubbered Kathy. "Will I ever see him again?"

Tilly handed her a box of Kleenex. "Don't worry. He's going to show up," she said, patting her sister-in-law on the shoulder. "This has to be a bad joke."

"No," said Maddy. "I think this is the real thing – a kidnapping."

"Poor N'yen," said Amanda, hugging her daughter close to her as if fending off abductors.

"Everybody keep calm," advised Jim Purdue. "We'll get N'yen back."

~ ~ ~

Agnes Millicent Tidemore got a steely look in her blue eyes. "Quilters Club, we're going to rescue N'yen," she vowed. Somehow, she felt as though she were responsible for losing her cousin and had to find him. That was the most important thing in the world right now.

"How are we going to do that?" asked Lizzie?

"Yes, what can we do?" echoed Bootsie.

"First off, let's figure out who might have a reason to kidnap him."

Oddly enough, Aggie had taken charge. The four women automatically huddled around the fifteen-year-old girl, nobody questioning her leadership.

"It's either a stranger or somebody with a grudge," postulated Lizzie. Brushing back her heavily dyed red hair, ready to put on her thinking cap.

Everybody knew that by "stranger" Lizzie meant "child predator," but nobody wanted to go there. Surely there were no such people in Caruthers Corners, they told themselves. So they went the other direction in their thinking.

"Who would have a grudge against N'yen?" said Bootsie. "He's just a kid."

"Maybe the grudge is against us," said Maddy.

"Us?" exclaimed Lizzie.

"Sure, why not?" said Maddy. "We've made a few enemies, I dare say."

"I suppose that's true," allowed the redhead.

"Okay then," directed Aggie. "Let's make a list of people who have crossed swords with the Quilters Club. Could be a bad guy trying to get even. Or the relative of someone we sent to jail."

"The Crackletons,"[1] offered Cookie. "They would be at the top of my list." The Crackletons were a crazy clan who lived in a nearby hamlet. The Quilters Club was responsible for three of Jebediah Crackleton's sons doing time at the state prison. Said to be inbred, locals referred to them as being "Cuckoo for Cocoa Puffs."

"How about the Indy mob?"[2] suggested Bootsie. "We nabbed their hitman, the thug who pushed that poor guy out of an airplane."[3]

"That's a good candidate," nodded Aggie. She and N'yen had witnessed the man's death, falling like a rock into the maw of Never Ending Swamp.

"What about Casper Crane?"[4] said Lizzie. They had sent the owner of the local antiques store to jail. The fiery redhead still held a grudge that he'd hired that mobster to kill her. Obviously, he'd botched the job.

"Don't forget that UFO weirdo,"[5] added Aggie. "He was in on the murder scheme with Casper Crane."

"No need to worry about Maurey Siederman. He got blown up in that Indy motel bombing," Maddy reminded her granddaughter.

"Oh, that's right," Aggie said, slapping her forehead. "R.I.P. to that flying saucer nutcase."

"Should we include Col. Perricock's son?[6] Jason wasn't too happy when the old man turned his mansion into a science and history museum rather than leaving it to him," noted Cookie. As the town's historian, she had been a direct beneficiary of that decision. Her office and exhibit space was now located in the mansion's west wing.

"Okay, how about Max Kasper?"[7] Maddy added another name to the list. "You know, the KemLab guy who tried to poison the town's water supply." No forgetting him. He had murdered her biological dad, Herbert Hoople. He would forever be seared into Madelyn Hoople Taylor Madison's memory.

"We didn't make the CIA very happy with that one," Lizzie pointed out. "Could they be behind this." The redhead bought into every conspiracy coming or going – from JFK to 9/11 to Spygate.

"The CIA does not kidnap American citizens," said Cookie. A patriot at heart, she thought better of America's intelligence community. They were on her side, weren't they?

"N'yen is Vietnamese," countered Lizzie. "And the CIA isn't very fond of Viet Cong. They were behind that war. Just ask Beau, he was over there."

"N'yen was born in Chicago," volunteered Kathy Madison from the sidelines. "And he's *not* a Viet Cong, for heaven's sake."

"What about N'yen's Uncle Võ?" interjected her husband Bill. "He was NVA. And he never approved of his nephew being adopted by a Caucasian family."

"Not a likely suspect," said Beau Madison. "These days Võ's a respected restaurateur in Cleveland." Beau's defending him was quite a turnaround for a former Army grunt who would've been shooting at Võ in the early '70s.

"Maybe he wants his nephew back," worried Kathy, glancing nervously at her husband.

"He's had plenty of time to assert familial rights," said Mark Tidemore. "I think he's low priority."

"Don't forget the Russians,"[8] said Bootsie. Last year the Quilters Club had broken up a Russian spy ring, believe it or not.

"That's right," exclaimed Lizzie. "The KGB plays dirty. Everybody knows that. They might kidnap a child."

"The *Komitet gosudarstvennoy bezopasnosti* disbanded after the fall of the Soviet Union," Cookie pointed out, displaying her photographic memory. "Its successor is called the FSB."

"No matter what they're called," argued Lizzie, "Russian spies are Russian spies."

"Could be our culprit is closer to home," interjected Maddy. "A few years ago we thwarted both the former mayor[9] and his nutty nephew.[10] Stanley is locked up in the booby hatch, but Henry Caruthers is still on the loose. I wouldn't put anything past that old crook." Mayor Caruthers had skipped town after embezzling half the municipal funds.

"Now, now, dear," cautioned Beauregard Hollingsworth Madison IV. As a direct descendant of a Town Founder, he discouraged disparaging others who had a link to the original settlers – that is, members of the Caruthers and Jinks and Madison families. Sort of like an Old Boys Club.

"At any rate, Stinky Caruthers – Stanley, that is – is out of the picture," said Bootsie. "He's still locked up in the state mental hospital."

"I've got another one. How about that guy who killed Boyd Aitkens' son?"[11] said Lizzie, referring to a long-ago fight over the Wilkins Witch Quilt. That quilt now hung in the Hoople Quilting Heritage Museum. "He might blame us for getting arrested. He barely escaped a murder charge."

"Bern Bjorn? He and his girlfriend Becky left town right after the trial," Beau reminded them. "I suspect they're gone for good." Rebecca Marsch had been Beau's secretary back when he was mayor. She was said to be a distant relative of Mad Matilda Wilkins, the aforementioned witch. But he'd never observed any magical powers.

Maisie Walters had yet another suggestion. "I think we should add the Blickensderfer brothers[12] to the list. They're probably out of juvenile detention by now." She'd always found these two teenage punks threatening. With good reason; they had been running a local burglary ring.

"What about –?" Lizzie began.

Mark Tidemore held up his hand as a signal for them to hold up. "That's probably enough names to start with. You gals may have been doing your civic duty, but it sounds like you've sure made a lot of enemies in the process."

"Funny about that," said Aggie. "How doing good makes bad people angry."

Chapter Twenty

Have You Seen This Child?

Everyone sprang onto action.

Jim Purdue left to join Myrtle Dobbler at the Police Department. He and the dispatcher would coordinate the roadblocks. His deputies had been instructed to search every single vehicle leaving town. By securing all the exits of the small municipality, they hoped to box in the perp.

Freddie Madison's firemen already were going door-to-door. Many of the volunteers had recruited friends and neighbors to join them. About two dozen in all. They had divided the town into quadrants and were steadily working their way down each block, swarming the tree-shrouded streets like an upsurge of 17-year locusts.

Mark phoned Lucius Plancus, a reporter with WZUR, a small AM station down near Pitsville, and asked him to get the word out about the missing boy. WZUR was the most-listened-to station in Caruthers County. Plancus promised to have the story on the air within a half hour.

Beau and Edgar decided to patrol the river. Most weekends they took N'yen fishing on the Wabash. If he escaped his captor, the boy might go to familiar territory. Maddy was afraid her husband might be putting his head in the sand, unable to deal with the idea of his grandson coming to harm. But Beau insisted he was following protocol. They had designated a spot under the Highway 101 bridge to regroup if anyone ever got lost or separated on a fishing trip.

Deputy Petie Hitzer was assigned to look for potential witnesses at the Town Square, the last place N'yen Madison had been seen. A difficult assignment, in that hordes of kids came and went across the Square after school every day. Some hung out at the bandstand, jamming on their 6-string guitars. Others played pick-up stickball in the grassy space across from the Town Hall. And the ancient 16-gondola Ferris wheel always had a serpentine line of customers waiting for a ride (at the everyday price of ten-cents a ticket).

Working his way around the park, Petie found two kids who remembered seeing the Asian boy, but they said he'd been alone. The operator who ran the Ferris wheel knew N'yen by sight but didn't recall him riding the big wheel today. Petie took one spin himself, just to survey the neighborhood from on high, the Ferris wheel being the tallest structure in town other than a couple of church steeples. Unfortunately, it was now getting dark and visibility was limited. It was hard to tell one kid from another at that height.

Ben Bentley's Badger Patrol was putting up HAVE YOU SEEN THIS CHILD? posters, the broadsheets on every fence, tree or telephone pole, blanketing the town with N'yen's photo. Each youngster was required to be accompanied by a parent or other adult to insure his safety. No one was taking any chances that another kid might go missing.

Donald Smyth and Buddy were plastering posters on every telephone pole and lamppost west of the post office. They had covered most of their assigned area shortly after dark

Hank Yager and George had been working the area south of the E-Z Chair factory. Predictably, Hank was belittling his son for not getting the posters straight enough. He was a terrible father, in most people's opinions.

Bobby Bjorn's dad was hanging posters alone, his son home in bed with an allergy attack. Ragweed season was just starting.

Dozens of others were out with flashlights, calling N'yen's name. Shadowy figures moving in the dark, it could have been Halloween night.

Back at the Madison's, Tilly and Amanda were watching after the little kids and consoling Bill and Kathy. N'yen's parents weren't taking his disappearance very well, just as one might expect.

"What did that note mean?" sniffled Kathy. "Saying that N'yen would be safer with his kidnapper. Safer than with *us*?"

"Just crazy rambling," said Bill. "Ignore it."

Tilly was looking at it the other way around. Who would consider himself N'yen's protector?

~ ~ ~

The Quilters Club had congregated in the Madison's spacious den, their unofficial Situation Room. However, Maddy wasn't the one conducting the meeting. The status was mindful of that Biblical passage, Isaiah 11:6-9, the verse that said "... a little child shall lead them."

At fifteen, Aggie didn't consider herself a child. But clearly, she was leading the meeting, determined to get her cousin back. "Let's narrow down the list of suspects," she spoke in a firm, authoritative voice. "We'll rate them one to ten, ten being a major suspect."

Lizzie had written all the names onto a notepad labeled TODAY'S TO-DO LIST that she'd rescued from the fridge door, but Cookie recited them from memory:

"The Crackletons?" she said loudly.

"Ten," said everyone in unison. No question, the crazy clan was at the top of the list.

"The Mob?"

"Eight," "Seven," "Six," "Seven," came the varied rankings. An average of seven. The Mob stayed on the list.

Maddy noticed that Aggie wasn't voting, instead presiding over the winnowing of the list like an abstaining judge. Perhaps feeling guilty. *Nemo debet esse judex in propria causa*, as the saying goes. No one should be a judge in their own case.

"Casper Crane, the antiques shop owner?"

"Five," "Six," "Three," "Four."

"He's a snake, but still in jail," Bootsie pointed out. "I doubt he's much of a threat."

"He was mean to me and N'yen," said Aggie. "And he wouldn't let my dog Tige come in his shop."

"That's hardly a reason to think he'd kidnap your cousin," replied her grandmother.

"I guess that's true," the girl admitted. "Take him off the list."

Cookie pushed on. "Jason Perricock and his henchman?" she intoned.

"Five," "Four," "Two," "Two."

"Off the list," Aggie decreed.

"Max Kasper, the botulism guy?"

"Two, "One," "Four," "Two."

"The CIA took him away," noted Maddy. "Doubt he'll ever be heard from again."

"How about the CIA itself?"

"Ten," said Lizzie.

"One," "Two," "One," responded the others. Not a high priority.

"What a flag-waving group you are," said Lizzie. Miffed at being outvoted.

"N'yen's Uncle Võ?"

"One," "Zero," "One," "Two."

They let it go at that. No sneak attack from the North Vietnamese.

"The KGB or FSB?"

"Two," Four," "Three," "Four."

"I don't trust those Russians," said Lizzie, "but I doubt they're involved in this."

"Agreed," everybody nodded.

Cookie continued the countdown: "Former Mayor Henry Caruthers?"

"Five," "Seven," "Six," "Eight."

"I wouldn't put anything past that crook," said Maddy pointedly.

"He's a bad apple," agreed Bootsie. "Still on the lam from the FBI."

"On the list," decided Aggie.

"Moving right along – Bern Bjorn, the guy who killed Charlie Aitkens?"

"One," "Three," "One," "Two."

Bjorn didn't seem like a vengeful guy. Just a grifter who got caught on the wrong side of the law.

"The Blickensderfer brothers?"

"Two," "One," "Two," "Two."

Maisie would have voted them higher. She'd always been intimidated by those boys.

Aggie had been keeping tally. "Okay, we'll keep the Cuckoo Crackletons, the Indy Mob, and Henry Caruthers on the list. Everybody else goes on the back burner."

"Now what?" said Lizzie. Awaiting instructions. An example of the mentor having become the pupil.

"Aunt Liz, you look into the Crackletons. Granny knows you. Go see her; she's the head of the clan. See what she has to say."

"That crazy old crone is nearly a hundred years old," replied the redhead. "Surely she can't be the kidnapper. Besides, didn't you say you saw N'yen with a man?"

"Granny has lots of relatives," Aggie reminded her."

"Okay, a good point. I'll drive out to Crackleton Corners right now and talk with her. I hope she hasn't gone to bed yet."

"Who for me?" asked Maddy.

"Grammy, you get the Mob."

"What? I don't know any mobsters."

"Sure, you do," replied the girl. "Barnabas Soltairé, the man who administers the Hoople Quadruplet Trust Fund. Didn't he used to be a Mob lawyer."

"Well, yes, but —"

Aggie didn't wait before moving on. "Aunt Cookie, you get Henry Caruthers."

"That dirty weasel? How can I possibly check on him? He's been a fugitive from justice for several years now. If the FBI can't find him, how can I?"

"Henry Caruthers has a long family history, being descended from one of the Town Founders. Take a look at your genealogy charts. Maybe you can find a relative who has an idea what he's up to."

"Not a bad plan. You've got it, dear," said the blonde historian. All but saluting.

Bootsie raised her hand, as if in a classroom. "What about me?" she asked. Not wanting to be left out.

"Lucky you – you get everybody else."

"Who's left? We covered the top suspects."

"You get all the discarded suspects. Can't hurt to poke around, just to be certain they're not up to anything."

"How would I go about that?"

"Several of them are still in prison. You can use the Police Department's computer to check on their status. Easy-peasy."

"Myrtle Doppler won't let me anywhere near that computer."

"Sure, she will. Your husband is her boss again. She wouldn't dare tell you no."

"But Jim would."

"Somehow I doubt you're going to be asking Uncle Jim."

Chapter Twenty-One
Granny and Jeb

G ranny Crackleton was sitting on her front porch sipping on a Big Red soda pop when Lizzie Ridenour pulled up in her new Mercedes-Benz E 400 4Matic, a $58,900 birthday gift to herself.

In the phosphorescent glow of a pole light, Granny studied the fancy automobile, but didn't appear particularly impressed by this ostentatious display of wealth. Everybody knew the Ridenours were rich. After all, this woman's husband used to be president of the local bank. Wasn't that like having your own candy jar?

"Mrs. Crackleton, good to see you again," Lizzie waved as she stepped out of the car, careful where she placed her Jimmy Choos. They matched her red outfit, which matched her red hair.

"What brings you out here this time o' night?" the old woman asked. Given the hour – 9:45 p.m. – she knew it wasn't a social visit. The convenience store across the street had been closed for more than a half hour now, and most people hereabout had gone to bed or settled in to watch TV. Granny suffered from insomnia, so it was not unusual that she was still up and sitting on her porch.

"One of our children is missing. Somebody spotted him up this way," she exaggerated the truth. Easing her way into the conversation.

"Which kid you lost?"

"N'yen Madison."

119

"That li'l China boy?"

"He's Vietnamese."

"Same difference. A slant eye. Really smart, as I recall."

"That's him. Do you know where he might be?"

"Lordy, no. Why would I know where t' find that li'l booger?"

Lizzie hesitated with her response. "Somebody said you Crackletons might have a grudge against the Madisons for putting your grandsons in jail. That you might be holding their grandson as payback."

"Haw," the old woman laughed. "That rich."

"Yes, but –"

"Sure, we Crackletons are unhappy with the Madisons. And with the Purdues. And the Bentleys. And you Ridenours too. All you so-called Quilters Club folks. But that don't mean we go snatching li'l yellow-skin boys."

"Nobody's suggesting –"

"Don't give me that. You're up here in the middle of the night asking if we got that boy. Well, let me tell you straight and true that we Crackletons don't have him." The old woman reached up to yank on a cord. A bell rang somewhere in the distance.

Lizzie said, "There would be a generous reward for N'yen Madison's return."

"How much?"

Lizzie didn't hesitate. "Ten thousand dollars." She was thinking, she had that much loose change in her checking account. She could afford it ... and would gladly pay it out of her own pocket for N'yen's safe return. Her husband Edgar had grown very fond of his little fishing partner.

"Now that gets my attention. First thing in the morning, I'm gonna put the word out among the family. Tell everybody t' keep their eyes open. Sure could use ten thousand dollars. Got big legal bills left over from my three grandsons. Ran up $80,000 in lawyer fees an' they still went to jail."

"Sorry about that."

"Don't give me any cow poop. All you hoity-toity townsfolk wish we Crackletons didn't exist. We're a big embarrassment to you leading citizens."

"No, that's not –"

Just then an incredibly tall figure emerged from the shadows. "Did you ring your bell, mama?" the specter said in a deep voice.

"Yes, I did."

"You know the convenience store's closed for the night. But I was working late, so I brought you another soda pop." He held up a big red bottle.

"Wasn't why I was calling you, Jeb. As you can see, we got us a visitor. This is that Ridenour lady who runs the new quilting museum."

"Yessum, I recognize her by the red hair. We don't have many carrot tops 'round here." Red hair was a recessive gene, lost in all the intertwined Crackleton ancestry.

Lizzie was getting nervous. She should have asked Edgar to ride out here with her. She recognized the giant-sized man as Jebediah Crackleton, Granny's son. Some people claimed he was the tallest man in the state of Indiana. Everybody knew he was a usurious loan shark, one shade short of being a local criminal kingpin. He'd once pulled a gun on Lizzie and her Quilters Club pals. Was she in danger now?

Granny continued on. "She just offered me ten thousand dollars if I could help her find a missing child. Have you got him?"

"Got who?"

"That little China boy what lives with the Madisons."

Jeb cocked his head to stare at his mother. She was showing signs of senility lately, no big surprise at 98. "I believe that boy's Vietnamese," he said.

"Same difference," she repeated.

"Well, I ain't seen him. But I'd sell the boy back for ten grand if I had him, you can be sure as daybreak about that."

Lizzie forced a smile. "If you happen to come across N'yen Madison, the offer still stands," she said, backing toward her car. Despite the phosphorous pole light, it was pretty dark out here in the countryside.

"Don't go running off," Jeb Crackleton said. "Sit on the porch an' visit. You can have this Big Red soda to sip on." He held up the bottle he'd brought over for Granny Crackleton.

"Yes, join me here on the porch," coaxed Granny. "Take that hardback rocker over there. We can get t' know each other better."

"Gotta run," said Lizzie, hopping into her car and starting it up. "Let me know if you catch sight of the missing Madison boy."

"Ten grand?" queried Granny.

"Yes, but he has to be safe."

"See what we can do," grinned Jeb Crackleton. Greed washing over his elongated face like a blush.

They watched as the Mercedes-Benz sped away.

"She's a mite finicky," observed the 6-foot-11 giant.

"So she is. But we can make us a bundle of money if we can find that kid. Or a reasonable facsimile thereof."

Chapter Twenty-Two
Mobbed Up

"Nice to hear from you, Mrs. Madison," said the baritone voice on the telephone. As smooth as melted butter poured over lobster. Cultured, controlled, confident. "This is kind of late for you to be calling. Are you having any problem with your trust fund?"

"N-no, none at all," sputtered Maddy. She'd been caught off guard that the receptionist had put her straight through to Barnabas Soltairé without any officious runaround. Being part of the Hoople family – even as an illegitimate offspring of ol' Herbie Hoople – had its advantages.

"Good to hear," he said. He sounded as calm as a psychiatrist talking a patient off a bridge. "Tell me, what can I do for you tonight?"

"This is a little delicate –"

"I'm used to delicate questions," he chuckled. "As an attorney, I can assure you that our conversation will be privileged."

Maddy blurted it out: "My grandson is missing!"

That seemed to get his attention. "N'yen? You're saying he's lost? Was he on a camping trip? A hike?"

"No, no. N'yen has been kidnapped. There was a note."

The smooth-as-melted-butter voice was now tough and no nonsense. "Do you need to draw ransom money from your trust fund? I can expedite that for you."

"There's been no request for money. That's why we're worried. I'm afraid this might be some kind of revenge against me."

"Against you?"

"Well, me and the Quilters Club. That's my –"

"I'm quite familiar with the Quilters Club," he cut her off. "Let get to the point. What do you want me to do?"

Maddy hesitated. "I'm thinking of your previous associates. The gentleman you represented before becoming administrator of the Hoople Quadruples Trust Fund."

"I assume you're referring to Salvatore Milano." Everybody knew Sal the Whisperer headed up the mob in Indianapolis.

"Yes," she confirmed. "Can you tell me if he knows anything about N'yen's whereabout?"

"Maddy, Maddy. I don't know what you think of me ... or of my former client. But I can assure you that Mr. Milano does not put children in harm's way. You can take my word on that. There's ... a code."

"So Mr. Milani has no hard feelings that the Quilters Club put his hitman – that guy Horace Greeley – behind bars?"

"I'm sure Mr. Milano will deny knowing anyone by the name of Greeley. But even if he did have any negative feelings, he wouldn't take them out on a child."

"You're sure?"

"I swear on my Mother's memory."

"Okay, thanks, Barnabas. Sorry, but I had to ask."

"No problem, Maddy. I understand. Would it help if I asked Mr. Milano to put his considerable resources toward looking for your grandson?"

"He would do that?"

"If I asked."

"Ask, please."

Chapter Twenty-Three
History Never Sleeps

After hours, the Perricock Museum of Science and History looked dark and forlorn, like an abandoned warehouse. As executive director of the Historical Society, Cookie Bentley had a key to the big stone edifice. Well, actually a key card – the museum's security system was computerized these days.

She slipped inside after deactivating the motion sensors and invisible laser beams. Using a purse flashlight, she made her way to the Historical Society's wing and let herself into the office. A crowded room that had once been a pantry, there was barely space for a desk and chair.

Flipping on the overhead fluorescent, she seated herself behind the oak desk (it had once belonged to Booth Tarkington, the Hoosier author who won two Pulitzer Prizes) and turned on her Dell XPS 27 computer. Over the past two years volunteers had created a database of practically every genealogy chart in Caruthers County. With a few clicks of the keys, she called up the charts related to the Caruthers family tree.

Every schoolchild knew that Jacob Abernathy Caruthers had founded the town back in 1829, along with the help of Ferdinand Aloysius Jinks and Col. Beauregard Hollingsworth Madison.

Henry Caruthers was a direct descendant of ol' Jacob. A few years ago he'd been mayor of Caruthers

Corners. But when the Quilters Club exposed his corrupt practices, Henry had skipped town with his secretary, Nan Beanie. The pair had never been seen since. Rumors abounded, the most popular one being that they were living in a fancy beach house in Belize on his ill-gotten gains.

Cookie went through the list of Henry's relatives, calling them one by one, asking if anybody had heard from the wayward mayor. The result was 28 big goose eggs. Not only had Henry failed to contact anyone, few would have welcomed it. Definitely he would have been *persona non grata* at a family reunion.

Comments ranged from "Good riddance to bad rubbish" to "He still owes me money." Relatives referred to Henry Caruthers as "a rotten apple," "a crook," "a scallywag," and "the last person in the world I'd let hold my wallet." Not exactly Mr. Popularity.

If Henry Caruthers were seeking revenge, he was going about it like a stealth bomber avoiding radar. Nobody had heard from him, seen him, or even received a Christmas card from him. The fugitive ex-mayor seemed to be gone for good.

Scratch Henry Caruthers as a potential suspect, thought Cookie, brushing back her dishwater blonde hair. No way he could be lurking around this town without being spotted. A foul-tempered little despot, he looked kinda like Mr. Dithers in the *Blondie* comic strip. With his photo having appeared in the newspaper so often, he was still a highly recognizable figure to local residents.

Gathering up her Vera Bradley handbag, Cookie was about to pack up and go home when she had a lightbulb-over-the-head moment. What about the ex-mayor's partner in crime? He's skipped out with his former secretary.

Nan had been married to Jasper Beanie, the alcoholic caretaker of Pleasant Glades Cemetery. She wondered if Jasper had heard from his runaway wife. Unlikely, but asking would take only one more phone call.

Actually, it took seven.

Jasper Beanie didn't answer at the caretaker's quarters nor at the Town Hall where he moonlighted as janitor. His favorite bar in Burpyville hadn't seen him since Monday night and two liquor stores swore he hadn't been in lately. A third liquor store remembered selling him a bottle of Wild Boar. That's when Cookie knew where to find him.

She phoned the Caruthers Corners Police Department and got Myrtle Dobbler. Because of the search for N'yen Madison, the dispatcher had stayed late to help coordinate the road blocks. "Is Jasper Beanie there?" she inquired.

"Hang on a moment," came the response. "JASPER, TELEPHONE!"

A few minutes later a tentative voice said, "H-hello?" Sleeping off another drunk, he was such a regular, the police didn't even bother locking his cell door anymore.

"Jasper, this is Cookie Bentley."

"How are you, ma'am."

"I'm fine. How are you?"

"Mighty bad hangover, I hate to tell you. Gotta start drinking a better brand of whisky."

Cookie cleared her throat. She was a little hoarse from all the evening's telephone calls. "Have you heard from your wife Nancy recently?"

"Uh, uh, no."

"Tell me the truth and I'll buy you a bottle of Jim Beam. The good stuff."

"F'sure?"

"Yes, for sure. Just tell me about your ex-wife."

There came a long silence, as if he were weighing his response. Jim Beam won out. "Yeah, she called me a few weeks ago."

"Where was she calling from?"

He seemed to think about that. "Nan didn't say."

"Is she still with Henry Caruthers?"

"She didn't say, but I think I heard him carrying on in the background."

Bingo! Cookie thought. "What did she want?" the blonde probed.

Jasper burped. "Sorry 'bout that," he said. "That Wild Boar didn't go down too good."

Cookie repeated the question.

"Asked me if I still had a ruby ring she left behind. It was her mother's."

"Did you?"

"You bet. Told her she could have it back. It don't fit my fat ol' fingers."

Here goes, Cookie thought. "Where did she want you to send it?"

"Nowhere. Said she'd pick it up."

Chapter Twenty-Four

Eliminating Suspects

Bootsie Purdue had been sitting there at the Police Department when Cookie called the dispatcher. On the sly, Bootsie was using the encrypted Panasonic CF-19 computer in Jim's office. The room was a mess, furniture askew, as if somebody were moving in or moving out. Jim needed a decorator.

The hour was getting late, but her husband was making the rounds with his roadblocks. Myrtle Dobbler was putting in overtime, the only one there except for Bootsie and that rummy Jasper Beanie.

Hooked up to the IDOC database, Bootsie had been checking names off her list.

- Casper Crane. Still serving time at New Castle Correctional.
- Horace Greeley. Incarcerated at Indiana State.
- Jason Perricock and his henchman Dietrich Tanenbaum. Both still behind bars, Perricock at Branchville Correctional, Tanenbaum at New Castle.
- Dr. Felix Pettigrew and Veronica Kardashian. Each still in Federal prison at Joliet according to NACJD.
- Stanley Caruthers. Locked away in Logansport, Indiana's oldest operating psychiatric hospital.
- Keith and Karl Blickensderfer. The brothers had been released from Indianapolis Juvenile

Correctional Facility, but according to juvie records they had moved with their father to Florida. "Gone for good," a relative told her when she phoned for confirmation.

No likely kidnappers here. And nobody with any associates to carry off a snatch, unless you counted mob-connected Horace Greeley. Maddy was handling that end.

For good measure, Bootsie checked out Jeb Crackleton's three sons – Dub, El, and Vis. They were still behind bars. Meanwhile, Lizzie would confirm Jeb's whereabouts. He was the one to watch out for.

Time to call it a night. Her eyes were beginning to cross after three hours in front of a computer screen.

And what had she accomplished? Nothing, unless you counted eliminating suspects as progress. She didn't.

"Thanks, Myrtle," called Bootsie as she closed down Jim's CF-19 computer.

"Far as I'm concerned, you were never here."

"Who was Jasper talking with?" Bootsie asked as she headed for the door.

"Your pal Cookie."

"Oh? What'd she want?"

"She didn't tell me. Just asked to speak to Jasper. Like I'm his social secretary now. Besides, I was busy getting your other gal Liz through the roadblocks. She got stopped out on 101."

"For what?"

"Speeding. Apparently, she got spooked. Claimed that Jeb Crackletons was after her."

"That'd be enough to scare anybody. Those Crackletons are creepy."

"Ain't that the Lord's truth. Crooks all of them. They'd steal a lollypop outta a baby's mouth, you ask me."

~ ~ ~

From the foot of the bridge, Beau and Edgar could see the red-and-blue bubble lights of the police car about a quarter mile up 101. "Doesn't that look like my wife's car?" said the former bank president, squinting into the distance. A full moon cast a yellowish glow across the countryside. This being Amish country, there were no lights coming from farmhouses.

"Naw, Lizzie's back at the house with the other gals," Beau replied.

"Yeah, guess you're right. It's just that you don't see that many Mercedes-Benzes around here."

"Sure is a nice car."

"I prefer my old Nissan." Edgar owned a '99 Nissan Xterra that he used as a fishing car. A compact SUV with a 170-horsepower V6 engine and part-time 4WD, the vehicle looked like it had survived a Yugoslavian endurance demolition derby – rusty, dented, most of the paint missing.

Beau kicked at a clod of dirt. "Think N'yen will show up here?"

"No, no more than you do. But it gives us something to do."

"You think he's still in the kidnapper's hands, don't you?"

"Pretty sure. Else he'd come home."

"Do you think he's been harmed?" Beau's voice broke a bit.

"No, I don't. The kidnapped called himself N'yen's 'protector.' He thinks he's taking care of the boy."

"But that's crazy. Protecting him from what?"

"Maybe from going back to his family in Chicago."

Beau shook his head. "That can't be it. Bill and Kathy are good parents, even if they've had marriage problems. And they've devoted their lives to helping kids. Bill's now the director of Chicago's Southside Youth Outreach. Kathy's going to join him there as assistant director."

"Yes, but with both them working day and night, who's going to be looking after our little buddy?"

"Maddy and I worry about that too. But we didn't kidnap N'yen to keep him from going back to Chicago."

"I know you didn't, Beau. I'm just saying somebody might have."

"Why would somebody do that?"

"Maybe hoping Bill and Kathy will come to their senses and leave him here with you guys. Where he belongs."

"I doubt there's some Lone Ranger out there trying to right wrongs."

"Maybe I'm just talking through my white hat, kemo sabe. Pay no attention to what I said. It's getting late. Let's go back to your house and see if the FBI has entered the picture yet. They'll find that little rapscallion. I'd bet an Indian head nickel on it."

Chapter Twenty-Five
The CARD Team

Special Agent in Charge Neil Wannamaker was sitting at the police chief's desk, in the very chair Bootsie had occupied twenty minutes ago. The FBI's CARD team had officially taken over the kidnapping case. Wannamaker was on his Samsung cell phone, directing operations with the fervor of a WWII general engaged in heavy combat.

The Bureau maintains five CARD teams strategically located throughout the United States. Deployed from regional offices, they can be on-site within one or two hours. Created in 2006, the teams claim a nearly 90 percent success rate in identifying and apprehending child abductors.

Wannamaker was there merely to provide support, for the team operated on its own like a well-oiled machine. The dozen agents assigned to the case meticulously followed the pre-established steps laid out by the Federal Bureau of Investigation Critical Incident Response Group's Child Abduction Response Plan.

Typically, one agent was assigned to liaison with the victim's family. He would verify the complaint information, develop a description of the victim, determine the circumstances at time of the disappearance, and ascertained the child's custody status.

Another agent would be assigned to assess the type of incident: abduction, parental kidnapping, runaway, or false report to conceal some other crime. But a disappearance is always treated as an abduction, until information is developed to suggest otherwise.

Other investigators would secure the crime scene – the Town Square in this instance – then begin collecting and analyzing any items of physical evidence

Additional agents prowled the grassy park, attempting to locate any witnesses to the incident. Those witnesses would be separated and interviewed, their statements compared to known information.

To Special Agent Wannamaker's chagrin, many of these steps where already taking place when his team arrived – interviewing witnesses, roadblocks, and door-to-door searches. Jim Purdue hadn't lost his touch, covering all the bases in a careful 1-2-3 order.

"Take your feet off my desk," said Jim Purdue as he walked into the room.

"Your desk? I thought you'd retired," the FBI agent jibed. The two men had always had a friendly competition – local cop versus the Feds. Kinda like a David and Goliath scenario.

"I'm back for the time being. Acting Chief since my replacement got murdered."

"I heard about that. Sure you didn't kill him to get your old job back?"

"Yeah, the pay's so dang good," said Jim Purdue, rolling his eyes.

"Need any help on that case?"

"Maybe. But first let's get N'yen Madison back. Some wacko thinks he's the boy's protector – or so the note says."

"Yeah, I saw the report. I've got a Behavioral Science guy on the way from Quantico. Should be here any time now. He ought to be able to give us some insight into the abductor's motives. No ransom was demanded, so the perp's aims are not clear."

"My wife and her friends think it might be a grudge again the Quilters Club."

"Don't tell me I'm going to have that gang of amateur detectives in my hair? No offence, Jim, but your wife and her crazy cronies could screw up this situation with their poking around."

"Don't worry. I'll tell them to back off. They're just concerned about the boy's safety. N'yen is like their mascot."

"Okay, but they've gotta let my team do its job. Without them muddying up the waters."

"C'mon, Neil. We've gotta get that boy back. He calls me Uncle Jim."

~ ~ ~

Beau and Edgar got back from their foray to the rendezvous spot on the Wabash, having come up empty, and parked the rusty fishing car in the lot behind the Town Hall. They had left their respective cars there. Being town councilmen, they had stickers on their windshields that gave them free parking at the meters.

They noticed a couple of black unmarked SUVs in the lot. A sign that the Feds has arrived.

"I'll leave Ol' Betsy here," said Edgar. That was his nickname for the fishing car. "Guess I'll head over to the fire department and see if the search team can use another door-knocker."

"Okay. I'm going to head home and check on Bill and Kathy. They must be totally traumatized."

"Tell 'em everything's going to be all right."

"Wish we knew that for sure."

"Take my word for it, ol' pal. N'yen will turn up safe and sound. Remember, that note said he was with someone who would protect him."

"Edgar, you're a good friend."

"I love that little rascal too. He's our fishing buddy. Caught Big Calvin, that danged catfish that eluded you and me for years. I don't want to see him go back to Chicago any more than you do."

Beau hung his head for a moment, choosing his words carefully. "Maddy and I don't want to lose N'yen. He's brought great joy into our lives. But it's only right that we let him go back to his rightful parents. Bill and Kathy love him too."

"Pshaw," said the retired banker. "That boy's lived with you and Maddy almost as long as he lived with your son and his wife. They've barely seen him in the last year, what with Bill working with those needy kids in Chicago and Kathy off teaching school in Cincinnati."

"Cleveland. She was teaching in Cleveland."

"Same difference. They left N'yen with you guys. Abandoned him. It's not fair to yank him away without so much as a fiddle-dee-dee or fare-thee-well."

"C'mon. Edgar, you're being too hard on them. They had a rough patch in their marriage. We were merely caretakers for the boy while they worked it out."

"It's not fair," said his friend. The bushy beard hiding his angry expression. "Maybe N'yen going missing will shake them up enough to reconsider taking him away from a home – a town – where he's loved and wanted."

"Doubt that's going to happen," said Beau, his elongated face reflecting sadness. "It's their call, not yours and mine."

Chapter Twenty-Six
No Girls Allowed

Nobody slept that night. The police roadblocks inconvenienced late-night travelers but turned up nothing. The door-to-door searches didn't yield any results, other than disturbing the sleep of practically every citizen of Caruthers Corners. The firemen and other volunteers had about ten percent of the homes to go.

The FBI's CARD team had rounded up some new witnesses, one who claimed to have seen N'yen standing near the Ferris wheel with a young man who looked like a Mexican.

Mexicans? Did that mean Boyd Aitkens was involved? Aitkens Produce employed most of the Mexicans and Guatemalans in this area, seasonal watermelon pickers who came and went.

Another witness said N'yen and his friend left in an old Chevy, an ancient gas-guzzler that spewed smoke in its wake. That sounded like a car a watermelon picker would drive. Nobody remembered the color. Nobody got a license plate.

The CARD team leader – a Special Agent named Brian Robert Winkler – sent one of his men out to Aitkens Produce, but he knew it was likely a Fool's Errand.

Special Agent in Charge Wanamaker reviewed the roadblocks and marked them with pushpins on the big map on the police department wall. He suggested a couple of minor changes, but all-in-all it looked like Jim Purdue had the town locked up tight.

Having worked all night, Deputy Pete Hitzer was catching a quick snooze on a cot in one of the holding cells. Jasper Beanie sat in the other cell, holding his head and moaning about a hangover that was off the Richter Scale.

And Aggie's dog Tige treed a neighbor's cat. He liked to play chase, a game that upset both cat and owner.

All of this before breakfast!

~ ~ ~

First thing that morning the Quilters Club marched down to the police station and turned the news about Nan Beanie over to SAC Neil Wannamaker. Not only was Henry Caruthers a suspect in N'yen's abduction, they pointed out, but he was also an on-the-run criminal, still on the FBI's Most Wanted list.

Wannamaker was unenthusiastic, noting that there was absolutely no evidence linking the former mayor to the boy's disappearance. Nevertheless, he promised to assign an agent to watch the caretaker's cottage at Pleasant Glades. Who knew how long it would take for Jasper Beanie's ex-wife to show up ... and even then, she might not have Henry Caruthers with her.

"We admit it's a long shot," said Cookie, "but it's the only lead we have."

"Henry Caruthers *is* a wanted man," Bootsie reminded the FBI agent. "Do your job – go arrest him."

"Now, dear, Neil doesn't need your help," said Jim Purdue, patting his wife on the shoulder. But the gesture didn't calm her down. She was like a skittish mare, practically prancing and pawing to show her agitation.

The leader of the CARD team asked, "Does this Caruthers guy look anything like a Mexican?"

"Hardly," Lizzie laughed. "Henry's a weaselly little white guy. Looks like that creepy uncle whose lap you never wanted to sit on at family get-togethers."

"Never mind, I'll pull his photo off the NCIC database," said the agent, a dour look on his face. No sense of humor on the job.

"I'm sure Jim's got one in his files," offered Bootsie. "For a while Henry was Public Enemy Number One around here."

"Got one right here somewhere," said Myrtle Dobbler, rummaging through her file cabinet. "Just give me a sec."

"Anything else we can help with, Officer?" said Cookie.

"Yes, anything at all," added Lizzie.

SAC Wannamaker gave the women an admonishing glare. He was a tall, imposing figure – kind of a Tommy Lee Jones type. "Thank you for your suggestions. Now if you ladies will go home and stay out of the way, we'll find that missing boy for you."

"His name is N'yen," said Aggie. Not particularly happy to be dismissed like this.

The CARD team leader looked down at his clipboard. "Yes, N'yen Madison. Also known as Nguy n Văn N'yen. We have it all in the records here."

Aggie was about to speak again, but her grandmother interceded. "Come along, girls. We need to go check on Bill and Kathy. I'm sure they must be quite frantic."

"But –"

Wannamaker stood. "If you folks will excuse me, I'm going over to the Town Hall's conference room to meet with my Behavioral Scientist. He might have some insights by now."

"I'll show you how to get there," volunteered the Police Chief. "I'd like to sit in if you don't mind."

"No problem."

Bootsie called after them. "Wait! Can we girls come too?"

"No," said Jim Purdue without looking back.

"Oh well, let's go have breakfast," sighed the chief's wife. "Maisie promised she'd be serving watermelon omelets this morning."

Chapter Twenty-Seven
Meeting to Order

The Quilters Club reluctantly moved over to Cozy Café, once again pushing and shuffling in an attempt to squeeze into the corner booth.

Maisie pulled over the extra chair to solve the seating problem. She followed that with steaming mugs of Maxwell House, freshly perked in anticipation of their arrival. Maisie knew her customers well and treated them like members of the family. As Maddy and Aggie happened to be.

"Any word?" asked Maisie as she sat down their coffee.

"The boys are going over to talk with that Behavioral Scientist. See if he can psych out who the kidnapper might be," Maddy told her sister.

"I can't believe it's somebody from around here," Maisie shook her head. Making the dark hair flop. It wasn't a very good dye job. Maisie did it herself.

"Yes, *the boys* don't need our help," said Aggie sullenly. Her feminist leanings bruised.

"Just you hang in there, young lady. They'll get your playmate back.

Aggie wasn't sure which irked her the most – being dismissed as a female, or condescend to as a child. So she said nothing and accepted a glass of watermelon-flavored milk without comment.

Didn't matter that this was a school day. Aggie refused to act as if things were normal when her cousin

N'yen was missing. Finally her mother had thrown up her hands and sent the girl off to caucus with her Quilters Club friends.

With Bootsie taking the spare chair, Aggie's narrow hips easily fit into the booth's seating next to the others. She snuggled in next to Maddy.

"Why did you let that FBI guy dismiss us like we were in the way?" Aggie whispered to her grandmother.

"Because we *were* in his way," said Maddy. "And arguing with him wouldn't help get N'yen back. Best we get on with our efforts without any diversions."

"Okay, I'm good with that."

Maisie hovered over the girl. "Want a straw with your milk?"

"No thank you. I'm trying to be environmentally responsible."

"Know what you're saying. I'm thinking of doing away with them all together here at the diner."

"I applaud that," said Cookie. She led a very "green" lifestyle. Some people called her a tree hugger.

"But I like straws," pouted Lizzie. "They help me not smear my lipstick."

Bootsie said, "I prefer Twizzlers. You can suck liquid through them like a straw ... then eat them. They're delicious."

Aggie downed the glass, giving herself a milk mustache. But she politely wiped it away with a white paper napkin. "That was good," she said. "I missed dinner last night."

"Here, hon, let me get you another," said Maisie, rushing off toward the milk dispenser. You could see an

Old MacDonald's Dairy logo on the dispenser's shiny metal surface.

Aggie rapped the tabletop with her knuckles – a *tap! tap!* to get everybody's attention. "I'd like to call the meeting to order," she announced with no further ado. Not even waiting for Maisie to bring over her watermelon-flavored milk. Getting N'yen back was the single most important thing in the world to her right now.

"Can't we wait till we get our omelets?" sighed Bootsie. "I'm starving."

"You can survive on a cup of coffee for a few minutes," prodded Lizzie. Still trying to get her friend on a workable diet.

"Okay, okay."

"Who has a report?" said Aggie, glancing around the table.

Cookie spoke up first. "You've already heard my research on Henry Caruthers. Let's hope the FBI nabs him when he comes around to Pleasant Glades with Nan Beanie."

"But you don't think he has N'yen, do you?" said Aggie.

"No, I don't," admitted the bespectacled blonde. "For one thing, I can't see him describing himself as N'yen's 'protector.' Can any of you?"

"No," said Maddy. "That old crook doesn't give a darn about anybody but himself."

"You're right. It doesn't sound like him," Bootsie agreed. "He's interested in money and power. I don't see either of those things going on here. There's no demand for a ransom … or anything!"

Lizzie shook her head. "Not his style. But I still hope the Feds catch him and Nan when they go back to Pleasant Glades to get her ring."

"Me too," nodded Cookie. "I never did like him."

Just then Maisie began delivering the omelets. Her cook was known for his fluffy omelets and other egg dishes. The diner did most of its business at breakfast.

The women began digging into the three-egg watermelon omelets, reminding themselves that nobody had got dinner last night – all those hamburger patties and hot dogs gone to waste amid the excitement.

Aggie rapped the table again, to restore order. "Moving on, who else has a report?"

"I do," volunteered her grandmother. Swallowing a quick bite of the fat omelet in her plate. "The Indy Mob isn't involved. Barnabas Soltairé gave me his word on that."

"And you trust him?" asked Lizzie.

"Yes, I do," admitted Maddy. "What's more, he offered his former associates' help in finding N'yen."

"You took it, of course?" said Aggie.

Maddy glanced cautiously at the police chief's wife. "Yes," she said. "I told him we'd appreciate any help his friends could give."

"I thought Mr. Soltairé got out of that business," muttered Bootsie. You could tell she was wrestling with the ethical ambiguities of dealing with mobsters.

"He did," confirmed Maddy. "But I gather he still maintains a cordial relationship with some of his old associates."

"Let's hope his friends come up with something," said Lizzie, willing to take help from any quarter. With the maiden name of Bergamachi, she wasn't fussy about the profession of certain Italians.

"Anybody else have a report?" Aggie looked around the table. Seeming very grown-up at that moment.

"Hard to say about the Crackletons," Lizzie remarked. "They claim they haven't seen N'yen, but I don't trust a word that comes out of their mouth. Nonetheless, I offered them a ten-thousand-dollar reward for his safe return."

"My goodness!" exclaimed Bootsie. That was a lot of money in the Purdue household.

"Maddy's not the only one with a trust fund," the redhead smiled smugly.

"That much?" Cookie questioned the largess

Lizzie shrugged. "That little scamp is worth it."

"Do you think we will hear from Jeb Crackleton?" asked Bootsie.

"I doubt it," said Maddy.

Bootsie looked up from her plate. "Why is that?"

"Because Jeb Crackleton is a greedy bastard. If he'd had N'yen he would've turned him over last night to collect the money on the spot."

"Jeb Crackleton frightens me," said Lizzie. "He's like a monster on stilts."

"He's six-foot-eleven," clarified Cookie. "Some people claim he's the tallest man in the state. The record seems to be held by John Wright, a man who was 8-feet-tall when he died in 1889." That eidetic memory recalling an article in the *Indianapolis Star*.

"Nothing to do but wait-see," Maddy concluded. "But I doubt they have N'yen. Else they would have offered him up for ten thousand dollars. Jeb would never pass up a sum of money like that."

Aggie didn't waste time on dead leads. "Next report?" she turned her attention to the police chief's wife.

"As my assignment, I checked out the B-list," Bootsie said. "Nothing there. They're all still in jail, except for the Blickensderfer brothers. But they've left the state with their dad."

"I don't trust those Blickensderfer boys," said Maisie as she delivered Aggie's third glass of milk. "They're criminals in the making."

"Yes, but those boys are burglars, not kidnappers," Maddy dismissed them.

Aggie slurped on her watermelon milk. "So, who's left?"

"Hate to say it, but I think we're out of suspects," said Cookie, a lingering disappointment in her voice.

"So what do we do next?" asked Bootsie. Her brown eyes wide and panicky.

Aggie sat there looking at her empty glass. "I don't know," she admitted.

Chapter Twenty-Eight
The FBI Profiler

The National Center for Analysis of Violent Crime (NCAVC) is a major branch of the FBI's Crisis Incident Response Group. This department investigates and researches violent criminal behavior.

Established in 1984 at the direction of President Ronald Reagan, NCAVC has become a national authority on serial homicides, rapes, bombings, child trafficking, and extortion.

Commonly known as Profilers, these agents draw on similar case histories to model the likely actions of a dangerous predator.

Special Agent Malcom G. Bradshaw sat at the head of the conference table reviewing the facts of the kidnapping. A Behavioral Scientist, he had flown in from Quantico late last night. Landing at Indy International, he'd been helicoptered to Caruthers Corners.

This morning Beau Madison had walked over to the Town Hall to check in with his son-in-law. This was a common practice, the former mayor conferring with the current one. That's how he and the Mark Tidemore wound up in the conference room with the three FBI men and Chief Jim Purdue.

Special Agent in Charge Wannamaker and the CARD team leader sat back quietly and let Agent Bradshaw run the meeting. Since arriving, Bradshaw had immersed himself in the facts of the kidnapping.

He was particularly interested in the note found on the Madison's doorstep.

"No one saw who delivered this message?" he asked. He was a beefy man with bushy blond hair. His eyes were as piercing as B-B shots from an air rifle. He wore a wrinkled seersucker suit that looked like he'd slept in it.

"I'm afraid not," replied Beau Madison. "When my son and his wife got there, they found it laying on the doorstep."

"Who was the last person to enter the house, passing over that doorstep, before they arrived?"

"Probably me and my wife," offered the Mayor. "We were running late. Got there around 5:45. My wife was putting the finishing touches on her egg salad."

"Egg salad?"

"That's Tilly's specialty."

Agent Bradshaw looked puzzled, but continued on. "And you're saying this package –" He held up the FedEx envelope "—was not on the doorstep when you arrived."

"That's correct," stated Mark Tidemore. As precise with his answers as if he were giving a deposition. The lawyer in him. "The step was empty at quarter to six."

"And what time did the boy's parents arrive?"

"At 6:15, I'd say," offered Beau.

"That's about right," nodded Mark.

"So this package mysteriously appeared during that half-hour time span."

"Looks like it," nodded Beau.

Bradshaw plowed on. "I've checked. Sunset was at 9:06. So it was still daylight when the package was left on the step. That implies a certain brazenness."

"The curtains were open. We have large windows," said Beau. "But no one saw a thing. No strangers lurking outside. No kidnappers hiding in the shrubbery. No FedEx delivery truck."

"FedEx didn't do the delivery," said SAC Neil Wannamaker. "We checked."

"This note is interesting," continued Agent Bradshaw. He held it up for all to see. A white sheet of paper was encased in plastic. Technicians had already dusted it for fingerprints, but found nothing.

"How so?" asked Mark.

"It's not a kidnapping note."

"Sure it is," argued Beau. Looking upset, gray eyebrows wagging with uncontrolled excitement. "It says this Mexican guy kidnapped N'yen."

"No, it says someone abducted him. This is not a kidnapping. There's no ransom demand. No offer to return the vic. Here, read the note more carefully." He held out the note for everyone to see more closely.

> I HAVE THE BOY. HE WILL BE SAFER WITH
> ME. I AM HIS PROTECTOR.

"I don't understand," said Beau. Looking extremely perplexed.

Mark the Shark spoke up: "It's like this, Dad. All kidnappings are abductions, but not all abductions are kidnappings."

"Kidnapping is the taking away a person against their will, right?"

Agent Bradshaw nodded. "That's correct, Mr. Madison. But all kidnappings must have *two* elements common. First, the asportation or detention must be unlawful – that is against the victims will. Second, some aggravating circumstance must accompany the restraint or asportation – that is, a demand for money or anything of value."

"There's no demand here," explained the CARD team leader. "Therefore this is an abduction, not a kidnapping."

Beau frowned. "But why would someone kidnap – uh, I mean abduct – someone unless they wanted something?"

The leader of the CARD team jumped in. "Child abduction is the unauthorized removal of a minor from the custody of the child's natural parents or legally appointed guardians. The most common cases of such abduction are divorce cases, where one parent has been given the sole custody of a child. In these cases the abductor is not holding the child for profit or any monetary gain."

"But there's no custody dispute here," said Beau. "N'yen was being rejoined with his adoptive parents."

"What about his biological parents?"

"Dead. An automobile accident," Mark supplied the facts.

"Any biological relatives?"

"An uncle," replied Beau. "But he's made no claim for the boy."

"We think the abductor is someone local," interjected Jim Purdue. "It's likely our roadblocks have him boxed in. He and the boy are likely still here in town."

Have the door-to-door searches turned up anything?" asked the Mayor.

"Nothing so far."

"Does the FBI have jurisdiction in a case if the victim hasn't been transported against state lines?" asked Beau. Still confused by this detail.

The Special Agent in Charge answered: "You're referring to the Federal Kidnapping Act 18 U.S.C. § 1201(a)(1) – popularly known as the Lindbergh Law. That makes it a federal crime if someone is transported against their will across state lines."

"Yeah, the Lindbergh Law," nodded Beau. "So how come you're able to help us here?"

Special Agent Winkler took that one. "Title 18, U.S.C., section 1201(g) provides special rules for offenses involving children. It gives the FBI jurisdiction to immediately investigate any reported disappearance or kidnapping involving a child of 'tender age' – usually 12 or younger. There doesn't have to be a ransom demand and nobody has to cross state lines."

"N'yen is thirteen," Beau said lamely.

"Close enough," answered SAC Wannamaker. "It's my call."

"Like I say, there's no custody dispute here. N'yen's parents *were* divorced, but now they've remarried."

"Not between the parents," said Agent Winkler. What about the current custodial guardians?"

"That would be me and my wife," scowled Beau. "I admit we hate giving him back to his parents, but would do nothing to interfere with that reunion. His parents are our son and daughter-in-law."

"What about someone getting revenge against the Madison family," proposed Chief Purdue. Trying out the Quilters Club's theory

"Not likely," replied Wannamaker. "The note assures us that the boy is safe and being protected. There's no threat involved."

"And no ransom or other demand," the CARD team leader added.

The Profiler inserted himself into the conversation. "Notice that the note does not say the boy will be 'safe' with the abductor. It says he will be 'safer.' One can assume he's protecting the boy from either the parents or the guardians."

"The parents, I'd guess," interjected Agent Winkler. "They were assuming custody of the boy. He would have been with them in the future,"

"That just doesn't make sense," said Beau. "Bill and Kathy are good people. Practically saints when it comes to kids. They run a children's outreach program in Chicago."

"Where's all this going?" asked Mark. Hackles rising. Was he going to have to put on his lawyer hat and defend someone – his father-in-law or his brother-in-law. He'd never particularly liked Bill Madison but he wasn't going to let a family member be falsely accused.

"Calm down, Mr. Mayor," said Agent Winkler. "Nobody's accusing your in-laws of anything nefarious. We're just establishing the perp's motive – rescuing the child from a perceived wrong."

"What wrong?"

"Removing him from this town."

"But who would do something like that?" muttered Beau. Almost as if talking to himself.

"Okay, Malcom," Special Agent in Charge Wannamaker cut in. "Give us the bottom line. Who snatched the boy?"

The Profiler paused to gather his thoughts. He brushed back his blond hair, shut his eyes as if reading some inner script, then began his robotic recitation: "I'd say a male between 18 and 30. Unmarried, lives alone. An ethnic minority who feels a kinship with the Asian boy. He believes he's protecting the boy from his parents. This is a single non-serial act, motivated by misplaced empathy. So the perp will not likely have a criminal record, which makes him harder to identify. He's probably someone whom the boy knows and trusts, because he apparently went with his abductor willingly. I'd suggest you try to identify someone among the boy's known acquaintances who might feel overly protective of him."

"You're saying he was snatched by one of our friends?" exclaimed Beau.

"Better a friend than an enemy," Neil Wannamaker observed.

"I don't have a clue," said Mark. A good father, he know most of N'yen and his daughter's friends. But he was coming up empty.

"This is going to take some thought," nodded Beau.

"Well," said Jim Purdue in a quiet voice, almost to himself. "Looks like the Quilters Club is off on the wrong track."

Chapter Twenty-Nine
The Money Demand

Elizabeth Ridenour's iPhone buzzed. "Hello," she answered, even though she didn't recognize the caller's number. "Who is this?"

"It's Jebediah Crackleton. You got that ten grand handy?"

Lizzie waved at her friends to get their attention, pointing to her phone excitedly. They were still at Cozy Café, finishing up their watermelon omelets. Everybody clustered around her, shushing each other, listening as she put it on speaker.

"Are you saying you have N'yen?" Lizzie replied cautiously.

"Put up the ten thousand and find out."

"How do I get the money to you?"

"Meet me in half an hour at the Bottomless Sinkhole. You give me the cash and I'll give you the boy."

"Okay, I'll be there."

"Don't bring no police or the deal's off."

"Whatever you want."

"Bring the money in twenty-dollar bills. Can you do that?"

"No problem." Lizzie paused, but couldn't hold her curiosity. "Did *you* take him?" she asked.

"Let's just say I found him," Jeb Crackleton laughed before hanging up.

~ ~ ~

Stitch in the Ditch

If you're the largest stockholder in a bank, it doesn't take long to get ten thousand dollars in twenty-dollar bills. Per Liz Ridenour's precise instructions, a dye pack was inserted in the canvas bag with the rest of the money. This ICI SecurityPac consists of a stack of real $20 bills with an ultrathin dye device wedged in the middle of the stack. These dye packs are used by over 75 percent of all US banks.

An explosion of red dye (1-methylamino-anthraquinone) renders the money traceable and stains the clothing of the person carrying the bag. A bummer for bank robbers and kidnappers.

"I'll call the Town Hall," said Maddy. "Maybe the FBI is still there meeting with their Behavioral Scientist in the conference room."

"He said no cops," Cookie pointed out.

"We need backup," insisted Maddy.

"Why's that?"

"Because you can never trust a Crackleton."

~ ~ ~

Maddy, Bootsie, and Cookie – Aggie too – piled into Lizzie's metallic-blue Mercedes-Benz E 400 and headed north on Highway 101. They were being led by SAC Wannamaker's black unmarked Chevy Tahoe, clearing the police roadblocks with a flash of FBI credentials. With him were five agents armed with Heckler & Koch MP5 submachine guns. The CARD team took kidnappings – and abductions – very seriously.

Apparently, they didn't trust a Crackleton either. Three of Jeb's sons were in prison for murder. This certainly proved the FBI's Behavioral Scientist wrong. Jebediah Crackleton didn't meet the profile at all.

Had the Quilters Club come through again? If so, Bootsie's husband was going to have some crow to eat.

~ ~ ~

As the two-car convoy neared Bottomless Sinkhole, the Chevy Tahoe fell back, letting the Mercedes-Benz take the lead. No point in spooking the perp. Lizzie spotted Jeb Crackleton's 1998 Pontiac Bonneville, a banged-up vehicle with a faded purple paintjob, parked near the edge of the sinkhole. She could tell by the silhouettes that someone was sitting with him in the front seat. "I think that's N'yen," she said to her passengers in a whispery voice. More a sign of nervousness than the need to keep quiet.

"Oh, thank God," cried Maddy. "He's safe."

Aggie gave a little squeal of relief. "I see him," she said.

Lizzie parked in front of the Pontiac. Glancing into her rear-view mirror, she could see the FBI vehicle lingering down the road, staying behind until she made contact. Hopefully, Jeb Crackleton couldn't see the black Tahoe from this angle.

"Hand me the money bag," she said over her shoulder.

Cookie passed it to the front seat. "But be careful," she said. "Jeb Crackleton's clearly a dangerous sociopath."

"Cuckoo for Cocoa Puffs," Aggie repeated the popular children's mantra.

"Don't do anything to spook him," said Maddy. It sounded more like a prayer than advice. "He might have a gun."

As Lizzie stepped out of the car, she could see over the lip of the sinkhole. The water was brown as a mudhole. Contrary to its name, the sinkhole was far from bottomless – twenty feet deep at most. A brick chimney extended from the placid surface of the water, a remnant of the house it had swallowed.

Jeb Crackleton slowly climbed out of his faded-purple car, pulling a boy along with him. There was a cotton flour sack over the child's head, like you'd see in an ISIS video. A symbol to indicate the boy's captive status. He seemed so small, standing there next to the 6-foot-11 giant. "Got the money?" the tall man called to Lizzie.

"Here you go," she said, tossing the sack toward him. "Now give me N'yen."

"Take 'im," he said, giving the boy a shove in her direction.

That's when things got crazy.

~ ~ ~

Aggie was out of the car in a flash, running toward the hooded boy. "N'yen!" she called excitedly. "N'yen!"

Maddy and Cookie were right behind her. Bootsie was struggling to free her seatbelt. It was a moment of chaos.

Jeb Crackleton reached for the canvas money bag. **CC SAVINGS & LOAN** was stenciled on its side. He was just opening the bag as the FBI's black SUV came racing up, sirens blasting. About then the dye pack exploded, covering the giant in red like the pig's blood in *Carrie.* "What the –?" he bellowed, jumping back, losing his balance and – as if in slow motion – tumbling over the rim of Bottomless Sinkhole. He hit the water below with a thundering *splash!*

Aggie was sobbing and hugging the freed boy. "N'yen! N'yen!"

Crying herself, Maddy enveloped them in a protective embrace. The Quilters Club gals – except for Bootsie who was still fighting with the seatbelt – surrounded them, squealing and sobbing. Relieved that the ordeal was now over.

With a trembling hand, Maddy yanked off the hood. The boy blinked his blue eyes at the sudden exposure to the midmorning sunlight.

Blue eyes?

"Is everybody all right?" shouted Wannamaker as he and the four agents poured out of the Chevy Tahoe, their MP5's at the ready.

"Yes," said Lizzie, taking a deep breath of relief.

"No," said Maddy. "This boy is not N'yen."

Chapter Thirty
Heard It On the Grapevine

J. Harold Wentworth heard through the grapevine that people had been making inquiries about him. A teller over at Burpyville Federal had overhead a telephone conversation. Somebody checking him out. That wasn't good … unless it was a potential client. But he usually chased clients … not the other way around.

He'd picked up one name – Edgar Ridenour, the retired prez of Caruthers Corners Savings & Loan. If he was poking around, it probably meant his wife and her cronies were involved. Ridenour had packed in his banking career for the solitary life of a fisherman. But his wife remained a member of that group of Nosey Parkers known as the Quilters Club.

Over the past few years Johnny had followed the exploits of those would-be detectives in the pages of the *Burpyville Gazette*. Foiling criminals. Solving mysteries. Heading off crooks. It never occurred that one day they might turn their sights on him. This definitely wasn't good.

He already knew the Feds were coming after him. Not much he could do about that. But he didn't have to put up with any pain-in-the-butt interference from the Quilters Club. He'd keep his ear to the ground. If he heard any more whispers of these snoops asking around about him, he'd have to do something about it.

~ ~ ~

Stitch in the Ditch

Tommy Truehart was oblivious to the kidnapping. He'd been too wrapped up in the murder of his cousin, Evers Gochnauer. His aunt was taking it pretty hard, crying and carrying on, a complete wreck. She was talking about selling the house, which would render him homeless. At $8 per hour as a stock boy at Dollar General, he didn't make enough to afford a place of his own.

Most folks would have described Tommy as a twenty-two-year-old slacker who led a fairly dull life – for the most part working at Dollar General and playing online games. He was pretty good at gaming, but that wasn't exactly a career choice. Back in high school he'd blown off the guidance counselor, never taking the aptitude tests. He'd thought about joining the military and becoming a drone pilot. That might almost be like a video game, shooting missiles at enemy targets and tracking Al-Qaeda terrorists.

Today he was late for work, the traffic held up by a roadblock. He wasn't sure what the police were looking for, but they were poking in back seats and making drivers open their trunks. By the time he punched the timeclock it was 8:35 a.m. That would cost him about $4 in his weekly paycheck. Shucks! That didn't help his penny-pincher budget. Maybe he'd just have a candy bar for lunch. At least he got an employee's discount at Dollar General.

Chapter Thirty-One
The Wrong Boy

The FBI agents managed to fish Jeb Crackleton from the muddy waters that filled Bottomless Sinkhole. Unable to swim, he'd survived by holding onto the brick chimney that stuck out of the water as if marking the location of a sunken steamship. However, in this case, it was the remnants of the Brandenberger house that had disappeared into the sinkhole in 1989.

"What do you mean this is not N'yen?" said Bootsie as she piled out of the car.

Lizzie turned toward Maddy and the boy, a puzzled look on her face. "No, this isn't N'yen," she said, shock spreading across her powder-white face. Lizzie always wore full makeup, even this early in the morning.

Maddy studied the boy, holding him at arm's length. He gazed back with a goofy smile. "Now do I get that candy Uncle Jeb promised me?" he asked innocently.

"I recognize him," said Cookie. "This is Faith Ann Ritchie's youngest kid. Faith Ann is Jeb's younger sister."

"He's trying to pawn off one of the Crackleton kin as N'yen?" squawked Bootsie, completely appalled by the idea of someone selling a child – even for $10,000.

"We got enough brats in the Corners," shouted Jeb Crackleton as the agents wrestled him into the Tahoe. "What's one less?"

"Tell me your name," Maddy said to the boy.

"Gus. That's short for Augustine. My mom said I was conceived in St. Augustine, Florida."

"How nice," said Bootsie. Not meaning it.

"My mom said I could go live with you quilting ladies."

"Sorry, hon. You have to go home," said Lizzie. No way she was going to take on more kids, her own daughters grown and moved away.

"That's right," said Cookie – the childless member of the group. "I'd love to have you, but your Uncle Jeb can't just sell you off. That's not right."

"It's illegal," stated the police chief's wife.

The boy stamped his foot. "Aw, rats. I knew this was too good t' be true."

"Agent Wannamaker can take him home," said Lizzie. "I'm never going to the Corners again."

"Sorry, but we've got our hands full with the perp," said the FBI man. Ol' Jeb was not going quietly, struggling ferociously with the agents who had just saved him from drowning. He knew he'd be joining his three sons in prison. Kidnapping – or even extortion – would put him behind bars for several years to come.

"Aggie and I can take him back," volunteered Maddy. "I know where Faith Ann lives. That little white house with the falling-down fence on Melon Patch Road."

"We'll drop you off at your car," nodded Lizzie. "Like I say, I'd just as soon not face Granny Crackleton again."

"Afraid the old witch will put a curse on you for getting her son arrested?" teased Cookie. Well aware that the redhead was highly superstitious.

"Those Crackleton scare the bejeebers out of me."

"Me too," said Bootsie. "They're all nuts."

"We'll get the boy home," Maddy assured them.

"But what about N'yen?" sniffled Aggie. "He's still missing!"

Nobody had an answer to that.

~ ~ ~

Back to the FBI's profile: The CARD team started developing a list of young ethnic men known by the Madisons. The list was short.

Bombay Martinez, manager of the local zoo, was Mexican, but much too old. The Madisons' gardener fit the profile pretty well, but he was visiting relatives in Guadalajara. One of the checkout clerks at Food Lion went on the list. Matea Davis got added. As did Deputy Petie Hitzer, although he wasn't ethnic.

Chief Purdue felt a little vindicated, but he was still worried about N'yen. Even though the Behavioral Scientist assured them there was no threat to the boy, Jim wasn't willing to take any chances.

An old-fashioned lawman, he wasn't entirely sold on profiling. Voodoo Science, he'd called it when having a beer with Petie Hitzer. People were complicated and crazy and impossible to predict, that was his opinion.

He was irked to see Petie's name go on the list of suspects. He'd known the Hitzer family for years – bought his milk from Old MacDonald's Farm. The boy was one of the best deputies he'd ever known. In fact, he'd recommended Petie over Evers as his replacement, but a small contingent of the Town Council – led by Boyd Aitkens – felt Petie was not seasoned enough.

Jim Purdue didn't want to lord it over his wife that the Quilters Club had been on the wrong trail – after all, they helped the Feebies nab Jebediah Crackleton. The nefarious loan shark had been in the police department's crosshairs for years, but always managed to escape proper punishment by the skin of his teeth. No way he was walking away from this one. The FBI's CARD team would be coming down on him hard. Nobody liked pervs who sold children.

~ ~ ~

Johnny Wentworth had had enough of those meddlesome Quilters Club biddies. He'd just learned that Maddy Madison's son-in-law had been talking with other lawyers about him. No way he was going to put up with this kind of crap. The anger was building in him like an overinflated balloon – about to pop!

He ought to take a drive down to Caruthers Corners and have a word with those troublemakers, he told himself. Johnny could be quite convincing when he tried, an aggressive personality trait that bordered on sociopathic. At least that's what the shrink had said. A court-ordered psychiatric evaluation when he'd been arrested for intimidating a witness a couple of years ago. He'd almost lost his bar license over that one.

Maybe while he was down there, he'd stop by to see his cousin Hank. They had a nice little insurance scam going. A local doctor was willing to certify any injury they wanted for a 10 percent cut. It worked out well –

10 for the doc, 40 for Hank, 50 for him. After all, it had been his idea.

The more Johnny thought about those Quilters Club women, the more infuriated he got. He'd "lay down the law" with them (he chuckled at the double entendre, him being a lawyer) and put an end to their nosing around.

But how to go about it? Then it came to him: He'd find that woman who was married to one of the Town Founders – Maddy Madison, that was her name. He'd put the fear of the Lord into her, as his granddad used to say. Threaten her and one of her grandchildren. That ought to do it.

Scare one, you'd scare them all! he told himself.

Chapter Thirty-Two
Enter a Guardian Angel

Maddy and Aggie stepped out of the convenience store at Crackleton Crossing, blinking in the bright noonday sunlight that tinted the countryside with a harsh yellow glow. They had just returned the Ritchie boy to his mother. Faith Ann had been called in to watch the store in her brother's absence — not realizing how long that might turn out to be. Jeb Crackleton was in Federal custody, heading for a 5- to 10-year sentence.

Aggie had insisted on coming along. Although a couple of years ahead of him in school, Aggie had seen Gus Ritchie at the Watermelon Days festival this year. An unruly ten-year-old, he was a juvenile-delinquent-in-the-making. She'd watched as he wandered from booth to booth, sampling the watermelon jellies and jams, gulping them down like a starving waif. And she was pretty sure she'd seen him steal a loaf of fresh-baked watermelon bread.

"Hold it right there, you two," came a gruff voice. A man in a blue pinstriped suit was lingering near the corner of the convenience store, blocking their way to the paved parking lot. He was big and broad shouldered — or maybe that was just the suit's padding. His dark hair was slicked back with a gel, Gordon Gekko style.

"Excuse me?" said Maddy. She was confused by the sight of a well-dressed city slicker here in this crossroads community, a place more accustomed to bib overalls and blue jeans than Georgio Armani suits.

"I want to have a word with you, Mrs. Bigshot Madelyn Madison."

Aggie drew closer to her grandmother at the man's hostile tone. This situation was turning bad, she sensed. Was this a robber accosting them in broad daylight? No, he was too expensively dressed for that.

Maddy stepped in front of Aggie, putting herself between the menacing figure and her granddaughter. "What do you want?" she demanded in a timorous voice. Now wishing she'd insisted that her friends accompany them in returning the wayward boy.

The man fixed her with a threatening gaze. "I'm here to give you a word of advice."

She looked around for help, but there was nobody in sight ... other than Granny Crackleton sitting on her porch across the road. But she couldn't count on much help from a 98-year-old woman, especially one whose son and main breadwinner she'd just got arrested.

The slick-haired man continued, "I hear you and your Quilters Club cronies have been sticking your noses in my business. Well, that's going to stop – right here and now."

"I don't even know who you are."

"He's a lawyer, Grammy," said the girl cowering behind her. "I've seen his picture on bus-stop benches over in Burpyville."

"You're a smart little cookie," said J. Harold Wentworth. "Be too bad if anything happened to you and your grandmother –"

"Nothing's going to happen to them," said a raspy voice from behind him. A broad-chested man in a jogging suit stepped around the corner of the cement-block building, a lumpy pouch in his hand.

"Who the heck are you?" said Wentworth, whirling to face the intruder.

"The guy you didn't want to meet," growled the square-jawed man with a pink scar running down his cheek. With that, he swung the pouch, hitting the lawyer on the side of the head. *Thunk!* The pouch — a man's woolen sock — split open, spewing a meteor shower of silvery quarters into the air. A homemade sap.

Wentworth went down like a sack of flour. *Ummph!*

Aggie screamed and Maddy turned to shield her.

"Nothing to be alarmed about, ladies," the scarfaced man assured them. "Just think of me as your Guardian Angel. Go ahead and get in your car and go home. You can pretend this little incident never happened."

"All right, if you say so."

"You don't hafta worry about this jerk ever bothering you again. After you leave, I'll have a little heart-to-heart with him. Just to make sure he gets the message. Wouldn't want to have wasted ten dollars in quarters f' nothing."

Without further comment, Maddy hustled her granddaughter toward the big blue Toyota Sequoia in the parking lot. Just before sliding behind the wheel, Maddy turned and called out to the mysterious stranger: "Please tell Barnabas Soltairé that I said thank you."

Chapter Thirty-Three

The Secret Place

"This is my secret place," said Matea Davis. "My true home. My *gumuk*."

N'yen was confused. "I thought you lived over on 4th Street."

"I rent a room at Melon Fields Apartments, but this is where I spend most of my free time." He indicated a dome-shaped structure, made with poles and cattail mats, covered by birch bark rolls. "This is my wigwam."

"I thought Indians lived in teepees."

"That's plains Indians. We Potawatomis lived in villages. In addition to wigwams, there was usually a longhouse for meetings, a sweat lodge for spiritual purification, meat-drying huts, and a ballfield."

"That sounds cool. What kinda ball did you Indians play?"

"Lacrosse. Teams use sticks to control a ball, trying to get it into a goal."

"Oh, like hockey, but on land instead of ice."

"I'm not sure," frowned Matea Davis. "I've never played a game on ice."

N'yen inspected the wigwam. It was about ten feet in circumference. Kinda like a large beaver dam, but on dry land. A wooden frame covered by protective mats.

"Step inside and look around," invited the young Potawatomi. "Home Sweet Home, to borrow a phrase from the *cmokmanuk* – the Whites."

"Okay." The boy peeked through the entrance. The room was furnished with woven rush mats and splint baskets. A central firepit provided for heat and cooking, but it wasn't burning right now. The room was dark and smelled of soot. But somehow it felt comfy.

"Nice," he said. "I'd like to have a wigwam."

"What kind of houses do they have in your homeland?"

"Brick apartment buildings. I'm from Chicago."

"No, I mean in Vietnam, where your people come from."

"Oh, my first mother told me she grew up in a stilt house. Built by her father, it was raised off the ground to prevent flooding. The house had bamboo walls and a roof thatched with elephant grass."

"We lived in frame houses back on the Reservation in Oklahoma. But I like it better here in Indiana in my little wigwam. Sometimes I can feel my ancestors gathering around me, whispering in my ear."

"You mean, like ghosts?"

"Spirits."

"This is really hidden away." N'yen swept his arms to indicate the surrounding forest – oaks and poplar and cedar, as thick as a jungle.

"My ancestors once owned this land. Now it belongs to a man named Elmer Jackson Wayne. He doesn't use it, so I do."

"Mr. Wayne died recently, Matea. The land now belongs to the Sons of Anthony Wayne."

"Your camping organization?"

"Yes."

"Ah, I believe you are a lieutenant colonel in the Badger Patrol, right?"

"I am."

"Does that mean the land partly belongs to you?"

"Gee, I dunno. I guess so."

"Then do I have your permission to leave my wigwam here?"

"Sure, I don't mind."

Chapter Thirty-Four

Potawatomi Legends

The night was dark and still. Time was suspended; it could have been two hundred years ago that they were sitting around the fire pit in the wigwam. The yellow firelight flickered on the mat walls, as if casting shadow puppets.

Matea Davis believed Yellow People to be cousins of Red People, so he considered the boy a relative. Thus, he repeated this favorite Potawatomi legend word-for-word just as his father had handed it down to him:

"The Earthmaker – *Kche Mnedo* – created the world with trees and fields, with rivers, lakes, and springs, and with hills and valleys," he recited. "It was beautiful. However, there weren't any humans, and so one day he decided to make some.

"He scooped out a hole in a stream bank and lined the hole with stones to make a hearth, and he built a fire there. Then he took some clay and made a small figure that he put in the hearth. While it baked, he took some twigs and made tongs. When he pulled the figure out of the fire and had let it cool, he moved its limbs and breathed life into it, and it walked away. Earthmaker nonetheless realized that it was only half-baked. That figure became the White People. The *Cmokmanuk*, we call them.

"Earthmaker decided to try again, and so he made another figure and put it on the hearth. This time he took a nap under a tree while the figure baked, and he slept longer than he intended. When he pulled the second figure out of the fire and had let it cool, he moved its limbs and breathed life into it, and it walked away. Earthmaker realized that this figure was overbaked, and it became the Black People. The *Mukte'nene*.

"Earthmaker decided to try one more time. He cleaned the ashes out of the hearth and built a new fire. Then he scooped up some clay and cleaned it of any twigs or leaves, so that it was pure. He made a little figure and put it on the hearth, and this time he sat by the hearth and watched carefully as the figure baked. When this figure was done, he pulled it out of the fire and let it cool. Then he moved its limbs and breathed life into it, and it walked away. This figure was baked just right, and it became the Red People. We call ourselves *Neshnabé*, the Original People.

"The Red People became many tribes, and they spread across the land. Among these tribes were the Ojibwe, the Ottawa, and the Potawatomi. They all lived as one people and said, 'We will keep this fire to represent our bond with each other, and the youngest brother, the Potawatomi, will be Keepers of this Sacred Fire. As the oldest brother, the Ojibwe will be Keepers of the Faith. The Ottawa, the middle brother, will become Keepers of the Trade.'

"And from that day forth, so it was."

Chapter Thirty-Five
The Missing Backpack

Breakfast at the Yager house was chaotic. Georgie was sniveling to his mom about leaving his backpack at the Injun Woods campsite. Their troop leader had hustled them out so fast that many boys had left stuff behind. A dead body will cause that kind of panic.

Emily Yager told her husband, "You've got to drive up there and get Georgie's pack. He's having a conniption over leaving it there. You bought it for his birthday, remember?"

"Jeez, that kid would lose his nose if it wasn't on the front of his face. I'm busy. Gotta go over the list of watermelon pickers with my boss. Boyd's a stickler for making sure everybody's documented. He voted for Trump, you know."

"Boyd Aitkens' business depends on migrant workers – immigrants," she retorted. "Does he want to build a wall to keep them out?"

"Wall or no wall, I don't rightly care. To me, them workers are no different than tractors and wagons – simply tool that help me pick watermelons. That's what Boyd pays me to do, keep the green melons coming to market so he can keep the greenback dollars coming his way."

"I wish a few of those greenback dollars would come our way."

"Well, we're not going to see any of them if I don't get to work. I'm late already."

Emily Yager planted her hands on her hips. Sometimes she could muster the courage to stand up to her husband when Georgie was involved. Their only child, he'd been a preemie and had never fared well without his mother's support. "Going out to Injun Woods won't take more than a half-hour of your day. It would make Georgie calm down. He's afraid you're going to yell at him for losing it."

"I might just do that," growled Hank Yager. But nonetheless he turned and went out the door. Emily could hear his Ford Ram 1500 pickup backing out of the driveway. He left rubber when his tires touched the asphalt surface of the roadway. The Big Horn Crew Cab 4x4's 5.7-liter V-8 packed an impressive 395 horsepower. Hank liked to display his macho status.

He headed up 101 in the direction of Injun Woods.

~ ~ ~

Matea Davis thought of himself as a *memegwesi,* a fabled race of people who hid in caves along the river. Old-timers of the tribe told stories of these *memegwesiwag,* saying how they loved children and would take them away from bad or abusive parents. A bedtime story handed down to Potawatomi children by their fathers and mothers – or a cautionary tale?

He told himself he was protecting his little friend N'yen Madison. Not that the boy's parents were abusive, but they did intend to take him away from this place he'd come to think of as home. He couldn't let that happen.

Matea didn't live in a cave, but his secret wigwam was located here on the banks of the Wabash, hidden inside this fenced-off forest known as Injun Woods. It was a good place to take N'yen camping, give his parents time to rethink their decision to take him away.

The *memegwesiwag* were supposedly bearded dwarfs. They looked more like the Badger Patrol leader, Ben Bentley. Although Matea was lean and tall and had a hairless chin, the spirit of a *memegwesi* resided within him. He had only needed a little nudge to bring it out.

That encouragement came from a rich white guy – a *cmokmanuk* – who offered Matea $10,000 to snatch N'yen Madison. But he had refused to take any money. Knowing they were joined in a worthy cause to save the boy was reward enough for a *memegwesi*.

Chapter Thirty-Six

Game's On

Back at the police department, Deputy Viola Fahrner was going through her locker in an uncontrolled frenzy. Although technically still on sick leave, she'd popped back into the station this morning, looking manic and wild-eyed.

"Whatzup?" inquired Chief Jim Purdue, stepping out of his office at the sound of locker doors clanking and objects hitting the floor.

"Viola's lost her badge," answered the dispatcher. "Thinks she may have left it here."

Jim Purdue had one of those illuminating moments – a light going on inside his head. Turning, he pawed around in a desk drawer and produced a shiny silver badge. "This yours?" he asked, holding it up for Viola Fahrner to see.

"Yes, that's it. Badge No. 305."

Jim Purdue mentally kicked himself. He should have recognized the number. The 3-0 meant nothing, but the 5 signified that Viola was the fifth deputy he'd ever hired for the Caruthers Corners Police Department. Old Harry Turnbull and Fred Altermatt had long-ago retired; that left only Evers and Petie and Viola.

"Where'd you find it, Chief?" asked Myrtle Dobbler, the dispatcher and major domo of the office. She hadn't seen a badge laying around.

"It was found near Evers' body. I thought it was his old deputy's badge. Didn't pay no attention to the number."

"Near his body?" said Viola Fahrner, shock showing on her nut-brown face. "Well, uh, I can explain that."

"Oh yeah?" said the Chief. "How would you do that?"

"Evers must have dropped it. He came by the house last Friday and fired me. Made me turn in my badge."

"That story doesn't make much sense," said Jim Purdue.

"Uh, why not?"

"If you turned in your badge, what are you doing down here this morning searching through your locker, thinking you lost it?"

~ ~ ~

Beelzebub666 had just now heard about N'yen Madison's kidnapping so you can imagine his surprise when he got an invitation on his iPad to play Tower Defense. He and the Asian boy had been battling it out online all summer. The boy was very, very good, but the player known by the avatar of Beelzebub666 had an innate talent that was hard to beat. Some genetic abnormality that made him a whiz at video games where the goal is to defend a player's territories or possessions by obstructing the enemy attackers.

INVITATION ACCEPTED, Beelzebub666 typed onto the keypad on his iPad screen. WHICH GAME TODAY?

A site called Kongregate offered 992 online versions of Tower Defense to select from. Over the past few months, he and his opponent had been escalating to harder and harder versions. Selections ranged from Defender's Quest (easy) to Royal Defense 2 ("The hardest tower defense game ever!").

LETS TRY BLOOMS TD 5, responded the words on the screen. I HEAR GOOD THINGS ABOUT IT.

OKAY YOU'RE ON! agreed Beelzebub666.

SUPER.

BTY WHERE ARE YOU?

INJUN WOODS … CAMPING WITH MY FRIEND.

COOL … BUT CAN WE DELAY GAME TILL I GET OFF WORK?

SURE, came the boy's reply. I WILL BE READY TO DEFEAT YOU AT FIVE.

Beelzebub666 typed: LOL GOOD LUCK WITH THAT.

Then the gamer put down his iPad and took out his iPhone. He called Ben Bentley, not sure who else to talk with. He wanted no part of the police. He'd been arrested for smoking weed earlier this summer. His cousin Evers had got the charges dropped.

He wanted to avoid having anything to do with the Indiana criminal system. Possession of marijuana is a Class B misdemeanor punishable by 180 days in jail and a fine of $1,000. He couldn't afford to lose his job right now.

The phone rang in his ear. B-z-z-z-z.

Somebody answered. "Hello."

"Is this Ben?"

"Yeah, who's this?

"It's Tommy Truehart. I've got something important to tell you."

Chapter Thirty-Seven

GPR

Dr. Howard Oakman and his wife Smithy hadn't heard about the missing boy. That's because they had driven down to Indianapolis to borrow ground-penetrating radar equipment from the Children's Museum. Having worked there before marrying Howie, she still had a condo in Indy, so they spent the night before heading back to Caruthers Corners early this morning with their Jeep Cherokee filled to the brim with the GPR paraphernalia.

Ground penetrating radar surveys are commonly used in archaeological geophysics. An electromagnetic pulse is directed into the ground and reflections of subsurface objects are picked up by a receiver. This graphs the stratigraphy beneath the surface, revealing any artifacts or solid objects.

Their boss – Dr. Henry Pendergast – had authorized them to map the subsurface of the effigy mound at Injun Woods. He had obtained permission from Ben Bentley, a representative of Sons of Anthony Wayne. Pendergast wanted access to the site before other archeological teams came rushing in. Running a science museum was a competitive business.

Howie Oakman and the former Amy Smithsonian had been students of Pendergast – old "Henny Penny" to them. Oakman was the more famous of the two paleontologists, having discovered a rare *A. magniventris* skeleton that the public had nicknamed

"Pittypat." But everyone agreed Smithy was smarter by at least a dozen IQ points.

They made good time driving back to Caruthers County, despite being stopped by two roadblocks. The police had looked into their car and then waved them on with no explanation.

The couple arrived at the destination around midmorning. They were surprised to see a gray Ford Ram pickup parked just outside the fence. Howie had a key to the gate because by now Ben Bentley had made several duplicates. However, he didn't need it today because the gate stood wide open. Lucky there were no cattle or livestock on the fenced-in property to wander away.

"Who could that be?" mused Smithy, studying the mud-splattered pickup. She noted an empty gunrack in the cab.

"Probably Ben Bentley, Cookie's hubby. He's the Badger Patrol's troop leader. I heard the campers abandoned some equipment up here. Maybe he's come to retrieve it."

"Think he'd help us carry this GPR rig to the mound? It's pretty heavy." Even though they were experienced diggers, Smithy was a slip of a woman and her hubby was certainly no Charles Atlas.

"We can ask. He's a pretty nice fellow. Donated the land for the town zoo."

"I thought Cookie was going to join us for this mapping?"

"She's supposed to be here by ten o'clock. Got another fifteen minutes."

"Unless she's already here with her husband," Smithy nodded toward the Ford Ram.

"Hmm, you could be right," he said. "Let's go see. We can come back for the GPR equipment."

Chapter Thirty-Eight

The Threat

"What's that?" said Matea Davis. "Sounded like a truck."

"I didn't hear anything," mumbled N'yen, not bothering to look up from his plate of scrambled quail eggs and fry bread. They were eating breakfast late. He fiddled with his iPad, pleased that he had service. Turns out there was a cellphone tower over near Bottomless Sinkhole.

"Yes, a truck," the young Native American confirmed his own question, quickly dumping dirt onto the campfire to smother it out. His manner suddenly turning furtive.

"Hey –" complained the boy. "I haven't finished my eggs yet."

The Potawatomi stood up, reaching for a walking stick that could suffice as a weapon if need be. "You stay here and finish your breakfast. I'll go take a look."

With no further word, Matea Davis slipped into the green wall of trees beyond the wigwam's clearing and disappeared from sight, like the vanishing act of a stage magician.

Unconcerned, the boy continued eating. He was hungry. He hadn't had any food since his hot dog lunch at school yesterday. Later today, he and Matea planned to hike down to Flynn's Texaco on Highway 21 and phone his Grampy to let the family know he was all right. The iPad still had a charge, but his iPhone was dead. His parents were supposed to take him back to Chicago today, so he wanted to let them know he'd be home this afternoon, ready to make the 200-mile jaunt from Caruthers Corners to the Windy City.

He liked camping out with Matea. Last night, as they huddled by the campfire, his Indian friend had told him stories of the Old Times, back before the White Man came, when buffalo roamed the land and the *Neshnabé* (as the Potawatomi called themselves) were known as the "Keepers of the Sacred Fire."

According to Matea, the Potawatomi were part of the Council of Three Fires, an alliance with the Ojibwe and Ottawa. Being the "younger brothers," it fell to them to maintain the fire that symbolized the confederacy.

Ka-bam!

N'yen's reverie was interrupted by a loud sound. Was that gunfire? The boy wasn't sure. The only shooting he had ever heard was on TV and in movies. Or at the shooting booth at the Watermelon Days festival – but those little .22 rifles made more of a *plinking!* sound. This had been a bigger gun, he thought. Maybe a shotgun.

Ka-bam!

Another shot. Was he in danger? He wondered if he should hide. In the wigwam? No, an assailant would look there. Maybe he'd be safer down by the river near the canoe.

Where was Matea? Was he all right? Had he been shot? Who was the shooter? A hunter – or the person who had killed Chief Gochnauer?

Was he about to become the next victim?

He was indecisive about where to hide. But then it was too late. He let out a shriek as a dark figure burst from the trees into the wigwam's clearing, waving his arms like a madman. Was that a gun?

"No, no," N'yen screamed as he ducked for his life.

~ ~ ~

Following Ben Bentley's phone call, the FBI's CARD team descended on Injun Woods like *shinobi* ninjas attacking a warlord's fortress. Four black Tahoes pulled up outside the gate, a trail of dust marking their arrival. The agents were surprised to find a dirty Ford pickup and a Jeep Cherokee filled with electronic gear parked near the entrance.

"That's Howie Oakman's Cherokee," Jim Purdue identified one of the vehicles. "I don't recognize the other one."

"Oakman is one of the folks from the Perricock Museum," explained Ben Bentley. "He borrowed a key from me so he could examine that Indian mound we found."

"Watch out for the citizens," Agent Winkler said to his men. "We don't want to shoot the wrong people."

"Be careful of any gunplay," pleaded the Police Chief. "Remember, there's a young boy in there."

Neil Wannamaker put his hand on the lawman's shoulder. "Jim, let the CARD team do its job. This is what they're trained for."

"Yeah, well –"

Already the agents were moving into the shrub pines that paralleled the barb-wire fence. They were wearing black Kevlar vests that displayed the warning: FBI. Some carried large duffle bags that clinked as they trotted along the parameter of the property. Weapons, cutting tools, flash grenades, no doubt.

"Okay, you know what to do," Agent Wannamaker said to the team leader.

"Roger," acknowledged Winkler. Into his mic he said, "GO!"

Some agents went in through the open gate, while others used wire cutters to breach the fence at three different points. Chief Purdue and Ben Bentley trailed behind Neil the Nailer as he followed the assault team down the path toward the Indian mound.

Twenty feet in they encountered the two paleontologists from the Perricock Museum. Dr. Oakman and his wife looked frightened. Perhaps it was the sudden appearance of men brandishing submachine guns.

"Quick," urged Howie Oakman. "We heard shots."

"Which direction?" asked the CARD team leader, his MP5 at the ready. Widely used by SWAT teams, the 9mm H&K assault weapon could fire up to 800 rounds/minute.

"Up there – toward the mound." Smithy pointed.

Agent Winkler spoke into his shoulder mic and all four of the two-man units converged on the effigy mound at the center of Injun Woods.

They were in for a shock. Atop the mound they found another body, stretched out like a discarded department store mannequin. However, unlike Evers Gochnauer, this one was still breathing. A 12-guage Mossberg lay nearby. Nobody else in sight. A large bump on the man's forehead told the story.

Two agents secured the inert man with plastic cuffs, not sure whether he was the kidnapper or not, while Winkler and four of his agents pushed deeper into the underbrush. Neil Wannamaker followed, his regulation Glock 22 in hand. Jim Purdue lingered behind with the frightened paleontologists.

~ ~ ~

Matea said, "Don't be afraid. It's just me."

The cowering Asian boy looked up, recognizing his friend. "What was that sound?"

"A *nashgin* … a shotgun. There was an intruder. I've stopped him for now."

"What do we do?" N'yen asked. He looked frightened.

"*Iwkshe' e'zha majigon*. It's time to go."

"I need my backpack. I put my iPad in it."

"No, leave it. We must hurry!"

He led the boy toward the creek where the birchbark canoe waited on the muddy bank. "Quick," he instructed. "Get in."

The boy climbed inside and Matea began pushing the canoe into the water. With a shove to get it moving, he hopped in. Positioning himself with crossed legs, Matea lowered his weight toward the bottom of the boat, then picked up a wooden paddle and gave a powerful stroke that sent the canoe under the wire fence that stretched across the tributary.

Within minutes, they were on the Wabash itself, moving fast as the paddle met the water. "*Kcumajin!*" he said, almost to himself. "Run hard!"

Chapter Thirty-Nine

A Hasty Escape

The FBI's assault team came upon a clearing with some kind of hut made from brush and bark – a Native American wigwam, it appeared.

"What the heck?' muttered Agent Wannamaker. The camp was empty, but they found a red backpack with an iPad inside. Evidence that N'yen Madison had been held captive there.

"Back here," called one of the FBI agents. "A creek. Judging by these scrape marks in the mud, I'd say a canoe was stashed here. Probably how they got away."

"Call out a helicopter," ordered Wannamaker.

"That'll take an hour to get here from Indy," Winkler advised. "We better pursue them ourselves."

"But we don't have a boat," scowled Wannamaker. "Are you proposing we swim after them?"

"No, sir. There are bridges near here– one to the north, another to the south." Agent Winkler pointed to a map. "Perhaps we can cut them off. Divide up, position men on both bridges. They'd have to pass under one of them."

"Good plan," said Neil Wannamaker. "Turn the prisoner over to Chief Purdue. Leave one man to guard this scene. Everybody else split into two units and deploy to a bridge."

Agent Winkler barked orders into his mic and there was a scurrying in the woods as the FBI men made for their SUVs.

Stitch in the Ditch

"What happened to the helicopter that brought Bradshaw?" Wannamaker asked.

"Had to send it back to Indy. They needed to repair some thingy on the instrument panel. Don't like 'copters myself."

"Well, get it back down here quick as you can. We'll need aerial surveillance with the kidnapper and his captive on the run."

"You got it, sir."

"Now how do we get to a bridge?"

"C'mon," said Ben Bentley. "I'll show you a shortcut to where Highway 101 crosses the Wabash."

~ ~ ~

The birchbark canoe cut through the water like a knife. *Slice! Slice! Slice!* – the sound of the paddle smacking the muddy surface. Points of light flickered through the canopy of trees as the craft picked up speed. The nose of the canoe was pointed downriver.

"Where we going, Matea?" asked the boy, holding onto the sides for balance.

"To your meeting place. The one you told me about. Your friend will pick us up."

"What happened back there?"

"An intruder. The white man who comes there to hunt, he attacked me."

The boy looked concerned. "Are you all right?"

"Yes. I had my walking stick. I whacked him on the head with it, then ran."

"Wow! This is certainly some grand adventure."

"Hold on tight. We must move swiftly – like the otter."

"The otter?"

204

"A *ktiti*, as we say in the Potawatomi language."

"I'm a member of the Badger Patrol. Does that make me a badger?"

"Yes, a *msuguk*."

"Do they move fast?"

"Fast enough. I can see the bridge up ahead."

~ ~ ~

The flat-bottom aluminum boat – a Grizzly MVX Sportsman – was a familiar sight for N'yen. He recognized it as his Uncle Edgar's. Tied up under the Highway 101 Bridge, it bobbed in the meandering water like a cork. Edgar Ridenour sat hunched over the bow, waiting, no fishing rod in sight. This was the rendezvous where Edgar, Beau, and N'yen had agreed to meet if they ever got separated. But Edgar sat here by himself, looking like a scraggly hobo in a $20,000 fishing boat.

Slice! Slice! Slice! – the canoe was moving fast, as if in a race.

The retired banker looked up at the sound. The approach of a canoe, its paddle digging hard into the water. He couldn't see the canoe yet, but it had to be Matea and N'yen. He leaned forward to peek around the concrete bridge abutment. That's when he spotted them.

"Over here," he motioned with an arm, as if sending a semaphore signal.

"*Ahaw, nIkan*," Matea waved back. Translation: "Hello, my friend."

"Hello, hello. Climb aboard."

Just as the birchbark canoe pulled up next to the jon boat, the crunching sound of tires broke the stillness. Multiple cars stopping on the bridge overhead.

Matea raised his finger to his lips, a signal to remain quiet. He drew the canoe close to the aluminum boat, keeping in the shadow of the bridge abutment. Hopefully, they couldn't be seen from above.

"Think they'll come down this way?" boomed a voice from overhead. Edgar figured it belonged to that FBI guy, Special Agent in Charge Neil Whatzizname — the one Jim called "Neil the Nailer."

"They've gotta come this way — or go north toward Highway 302," replied a familiar voice. None other than Edgar's pal Ben Bentley. "There aren't any easy places to go ashore between here and there. Briars and bushes and mudflats and steep banks."

"Any alligators?"

"Not really. Back in '05 three gators were spotted in the Wabash up near Huntington. But they were just someone's pets that grew too large to flush down the commode."

"Snakes?"

"No dangerous snakes. Cottonmouths can be found further south here in Indiana. Copperheads too. Up this way you see an occasional Eastern Massasauga Rattlesnake along the bank. But they're listed as an endangered species. Mostly you'll see harmless varieties like the Black Rat Snake or the Blue Racer. They're likely to be more afraid of you than you them."

"I'm not much of an outdoors guy," admitted Neil Wannamaker. "Grew up in Chicago. A city boy. You're not going to catch me sleeping in a wigwam or even a pup tent. I prefer a feather bed at the Palmer House."

While the men were talking, Matea quietly climbed into the jon boat and helped N'yen follow him. Then he deliberately tipped over his canoe and sank it. A single boat was easier to keep out of view if anyone decided to look over the bridge's railing. Hopefully, all the attention was being focused up the river in the direction of Injun Woods.

"Shouldn't that canoe be down here by now?" came Neil Wannamaker's voice from overhead.

"I'm thinking they went north."

"Well, now we know how the kidnapper got past the Injun Woods fence," the FBI man said. "The wire didn't come down to the water level on that tributary. A canoe could pass right under it."

"That accounts for the kidnapper," agreed Ben Bentley. "But how did Evers Gochnauer get in there? I didn't give him a key. And he didn't have a boat."

"Dunno. Not my case," the FBI man said. "I'll let Jim figure that one out."

Chapter Forty

Too Many Crooks

Chief Purdue was doing the paperwork while his deputy processed the prisoner – photographing him, fingerprinting him, collecting his personal items, and issuing an orange jumpsuit. Hank Yager would go into a holding cell, later to be transferred to Indianapolis where the police had proper long-term facilities.

This required a little juggling. There were only two cells. Jeb Crackleton already occupied one. And Viola Fahrner waited in the chief's office, essentially under house arrest until she could clear up the mystery about that deputy's badge.

So Yager got the second cell. No sooner had Deputy Pete Hitzer shut the barred door than he began protesting, "I'm telling you I'm not a kidnapper. I want to talk with my lawyer."

"Relax. You'll get to do that in due time."

"I know my rights," insisted Yager. "I get a phone call. I demand you let me contact J. Harold Wentworth. He's my personal lawyer."

"If you're not a kidnapper," snarled the deputy, "what were you doing up there in Injun Woods with that boy?"

"I didn't see no boy. I went up there to retrieve my son's backpack."

Petie had already Mirandized this guy Yager, but talking to a prisoner without his attorney present was tricky ground. "Yeah? How did you get in?"

"I've got a key, stupid. It's right there in that tray with my wallet and spare change."

"Really? Who gave you a key?"

"My lawyer – Johnny Wentworth. He oversaw the property for ol' Elmer."

Chief Jim Purdue looked up. He'd been shuffling papers at his desk. Keeping an eye on Viola. He walked over to the door and called to the prisoner, "You say you got the key from Wentworth?"

"That's right. Loaned it to me so I could go hunting up there," responded Hank Yager. "A gesture of appreciation for all the business I send him."

Chief Purdue scrunched up his face and squinted one eye. "Exactly what business is that?"

"Oh, I've had a few insurance claims. Slip and fall. Whiplash. I'm on partial disability."

Jim Purdue's blood pressure shot upward like a Fourth of July bottle rocket. "Wentworth!" he shouted. "That lying polecat told me there was only one key, the one he gave to Ben Bentley."

"Ha! That's 'tween you and him."

"You had a key," accused Jim Purdue. "That means you could've gone in there with Evers Gochnauer and killed him."

"You don't have any proof of that. I didn't even know that fat tinpot bully of a police chief."

Petie Hitzer grabbed the prisoner's collar and shook him hard. "Watch your mouth, you dirty –"

"Petie, back off," called Jim Purdue.

"But, Chief –"

"Don't worry, we'll get to the bottom of this. You can bet your bippy on that."

Petie Hitzer looked puzzled. "What's a bippy?" he said.

~ ~ ~

"Bippy" is a US slang word that's used euphemistically for an unspecified part of the body. Generally, it's understood to be the equivalent to one's butt.

Petie Hitzer didn't have much of a behind to bet. The deputy was skinny as a stick, his hips so narrow they had trouble holding up his gun belt.

Being a small town, Petie had heard of Henrik "Hank" Yager. A supervisor at Aitkens Produce, the man had a reputation for abusing the Mexican laborers. Boyd Aitkens was the biggest employer in the county, but the majority of his hires were seasonal migratory watermelon pickers.

Another thing, Petie had heard that Yager was an inveterate womanizer. No matter that he had a perfectly fine wife and twelve-year-old kid at home. At one time, Yager had a fling with that cute little blonde who handled the take-out window at the Dairy Queen. But he'd dumped her for another woman. She'd told Petie the sordid story herself, amid copious tears and several cones of soft-serve custard.

Being a good Mennonite, Petie didn't approve of such wicked behavior. He'd once mentioned it to Deputy Fahrner, but she didn't want to talk about it. Surprising, in that she loved gossip and TV soap operas and reading *True Confession* magazine.

Now Viola Fahrner sat fuming in the Chief's office, being held for questioning in the death of their former boss. How could that be? She was a good cop ... wasn't she?

~ ~ ~

The trio hunkered there under the bridge in Edgar Ridenour's aluminum jon boat, not saying a word until they heard the FBI man exclaim, "Could they have beat us down the river?"

"Possibly," allowed Ben Bentley. "Depends how much of a head start they had."

"Couldn't have been much of one," opined Wannamaker. "Those museum geeks said they heard two shots just minutes before we got there."

"But who was doing the shooting – that guy we found or the guy who made off with the boy?"

"Won't know till we interview the man we found. But my guess he's just a hunter who stumbled across the kidnapper's camp."

"Who was that guy? Chief Purdue hustled him off before I got a look at him."

"Beats me. Right now, I'm concerned about the boy's safety. They were obviously holding him in that makeshift shelter up there."

"That shelter was actually a wigwam," observed Ben Bentley. "A local Potawatomi recently showed my campers how to make one."

"Oh? Who's this wigwam maker of yours?"

"A fellow named Matea Davis. But he can't be the kidnapper. I'd trust him with my last penny. A good guy."

"We'll see about that." Wannamaker sounded doubtful.

Another agent said, "Matea Davis – his name's on the list of suspects we developed based on Bradshaw's profile."

"Yeah?"

The agent recited: "A twenty-three-year old Indian male. Could probably be mistaken for a Mexican. He was friendly with the missing boy."

"No, Matea couldn't be your guy," argued Ben Bentley. "He's been working with my Badger Patrol boys. Teaches woodlore."

"You'd be surprised how many pedophiles work for day care centers or as Boy Scout troop leaders."

"Hey –" Ben took offence at that. "I'm a troop leader."

"Don't get your bowels in an uproar. Nobody was suggesting you."

"I'm telling you Matea's not a pedophile. Or a kidnapper."

"Then how do you explain him being up there in Injun Woods with the boy?"

"Who says it was him?"

Agent Wannamaker leaned against the bridge railing. "Can't be too many people around here who know how to build a wigwam."

"Don't be so sure about that. All twelve of my Badger Patrol boys could build one in less than a day."

"You don't say? How old are they?"

"Twelve and thirteen."

"Not likely suspects."

Ben Bentley had had enough "It getting hot out here," he said, glancing at the overhead sun. "If that canoe was coming down the river, it would be here by now. We may as well pack it in."

Neil the Nailer looked around at the rolling countryside, the serpentine river, the razor-straight highway leading back to Caruthers Corners. "Guess you're right," he said. "Let's head back to town. Winkler can handle the search. I've called in a helicopter. They won't get far."

~ ~ ~

Waiting in the shadows under the bridge, N'yen was confused as to why they were hiding from the people on the bridge – wasn't one of them his Uncle Ben? But this was the rendezvous point he and Grampy and Uncle Edgar had agreed upon in the case of an emergency, and here was Uncle Edgar waiting for him and Matea.

Was this an emergency?

He wasn't quite sure why they were running. Had someone attacked Matea back there in Injun Woods?

He'd heard someone on the bridge say something about "kidnapping"? That couldn't be right. Matea hadn't kidnapped him; he'd only taken him on a camping trip as a going-away surprise. And here was his Uncle Edgar – his fishing partner – to demonstrate that everything was A-Okay.

So why were those people on the bridge chasing them?

After a while, he heard several cars pulling away, tires squealing on the asphalt above. That was followed by silence. Not even any crickets chirping.

They waited there, listening to water slapping against the concrete abutment. Crickets eventually began to sing again. The noonday sun reflected off the muddy surface of the Wabash. Edgar Ridenour exhaled his breath and said, "Okay, I think it's safe to go."

"Go where, Uncle Edgar?"

"Back home. I'm afraid my little plan has gone awry. Too many people are upset. I didn't reckon on that."

"Are we in trouble?" asked Matea.

"Stick to your story about an overnight camping trip and you'll be all right. I'll say you ran the idea past me and I neglected to mention it because I was so upset that N'yen was moving away."

"You were upset, Uncle Edgar?"

"Of course, I was. I don't want to lose my little fishing buddy."

Part III

"Among our Potawatomi people, women are the Keepers of Water. We carry the sacred water to ceremonies and act on its behalf."

- Robin Wall Kimmerer, *Braiding Sweetgrass: Indigenous Wisdom, Scientific Knowledge, and the Teachings of Plants*

Chapter Forty-One

Matea Davis

The Quilters Club got the word that one kidnapper had been captured and his accomplice on the run. The FBI thought the boy was still in the custody of the second kidnapper, but safe. That was a relief to everybody. N'yen's wellbeing being paramount in their prayers.

All morning Bill had been ringing his hands and pacing; Kathy was experiencing a shortness of breath. All eyes were red. They were total wrecks.

Doc Medford came over to the house and placed Bill and Kathy on a mild tranquilizer called Diazapam. Commonly known as Valium, this Schedule IV benzodiazepine derivative is prescribed for anxiety and panic disorders. Within 15 minutes the couple had mellowed out, enveloped in a drunken-like state and experiencing a slight sense of euphoria. Perhaps they had taken a few too many pills.

Now at two o'clock in the afternoon there was little to do but wait. The FBI agent liaised to babysit the family reported that the man at large was thought to be a Native American named Matea Davison.

"Davis," Maddy corrected. She found it difficult to image Matea as a kidnapper, nonetheless she felt a sense of relief. She knew that if N'yen was with the Potawatomi he would be safe. Matea would never harm his little Asian buddy.

"What do we do next?" asked Aggie, the wind out of her sails. Her leadership status crumbling. She found it difficult to believe Matea Davis was behind this.

"There's nothing we can do," responded her grandmother. "The FBI has a helicopter searching the area north of Highway 101. That's mostly open watermelon fields. N'yen and Matea will turn up soon."

"Are you sure N'yen will be all right?"

"Do you trust Matea Davis?"

"Yes, I like him very much. He's our friend. He made us Blood Brothers."

"Then you have your answer. Didn't the note say he was N'yen's 'protector'?"

That satisfied the inquisitive girl. "Yes. Yes, it did. Now if Matea will just bring N'yen back home everything will be all right."

Cookie wasn't so sure. "What do we really know about Matea Davis," she pointed out. "He shows up here one day, says he's a Potawatomi Indian from Oklahoma, and we take him in without any questions. For all we know he's a criminal on the run. A bank robber or a murderer."

"A bank robber?" said Lizzie. With her connections to the Caruthers Corners Savings & Loan, she was not fond of Bonnie and Clyde types. "What makes you think that."

"I don't," Cookie admitted. "I'm just worried."

Bootsie got their attention. "Hey, I just got off the phone with Jim. He ran an NCIC report on Matea. He comes up clean except for a ticket for trespass when he was nineteen-years-old. He was caught freeing a calf that got tangled in a barb-wire fence on a white rancher's property."

"He doesn't sound too dangerous," observed Lizzie. She may have had a mild crush on the handsome young man.

"Jim says Matea is a member in good standing of the Citizen Potawatomi Nation, the tribe that lives in Oklahoma. There are 10,312 Potawatomi in that state. Well, 10,311 with Matea being here in Caruthers Corners." Bootsie had taken notes from her phone conversation with her husband.

Cookie evoked her eidetic memory. "Federally recognized in 1948, the Citizen Potawatomi Nation is the ninth-largest American Indian tribe in the United States," she recited. "With assets over $111-million, the Nation owns and operates the First National Bank and Trust of Shawnee, KGFF radio station, and CPN-Net Internet Services. The Oklahoma reservation covers almost all of Pottawatomie County, half of Cleveland County, and a portion of Oklahoma County – some 275,000 acres in all."

"Impressive," said Maddy. She was glad to learn the Native Americans had done well after being forced off their land in Indiana.

"That's not all," continued Bootsie. "Matea's father is a tribal elder in the Citizen Potawatomi Nation. He helped found the tribe's two casinos, The Grand Casino Resort and Firelake Casino. He's pretty well-to-do for an Indian, Jim says."

Lizzie didn't want to be left out: "I happen to know that the First National Bank & Trust is the largest tribally owned national bank in the United States."

"Yes," nodded Cookie. Again calling on her super memory. "CPN purchased the bank in 1989. Today it has assets in excess of $230-million."

"However, that's not Matea's money," Maddy pointed out. "As far as I know, he's simply a young single guy who makes a below-minimum wage as a night watchman. Poor but honest."

Aggie's mood definitely brightened. "Now that I know N'yen is with Matea, I feel much better. I'm sure he will be coming home soon."

Bill and Kathy nodded, barely comprehending the news, still lost in a tranquilizer-addled fog. "Can't wait to get that little fellow home to Chicago," muttered Kathy. "Away from all these crazy six-toed people and crooked politicians and child-snatching Red Indians."

Aggie got up and left the room.

Chapter Forty-Two
The Safe Return

Ben Bentley and SAC Wannamaker returned to the police department. Neither group of FBI agents had spotted the canoe. It was assumed the Indian escaped with the boy by some other route, maybe some unmarked tributary in between the two bridges. A helicopter was on its way from Indy to conduct a search from the air. The fugitives would turn up soon, Wannamaker told himself.

"I've suspended the door-to-door search," reported Chief Purdue. "Your boys have the kidnapper on the run. He and N'yen are obviously not here in the town."

"I see you've got the accomplice behind bars," Wannamaker nodded toward the prisoner.

"Locked up tight as a tick."

Ben Bentley did a double take. "What the heck's going on here? That's not a kidnapper, that's Hank Yager. His son Georgie's in the Beaver Patrol along with N'yen Madison."

"That's what I've been trying to tell 'em," Yager called from the holding cell. "I was merely out there to retrieve my son's backpack."

"The boys abandoned most of their gear when we found the dead body," Ben Bentley confirmed. "I was planning to go out there and gather it up myself. But then N'yen went missing."

"Like I said," Hank Yager continued to plead his case, "I went up to Injun Woods to pick up my son's backpack when some maniac jumps out of the bushes and whacks me over the head with a stick."

"Did you recognize your assailant?" asked Neil Wannamaker. "Tall, short, skinny, fat?"

Yager paused to think, shutting his eyes in order to form a mental image. "More tall than short. In good physical shape, I'd say. Dark hair, dark eyes. Some ethnic type, a Mexican or Indian or Guatemalan. He was carrying a club of some type. Attacked me without provocation."

"That sounds like the guy described by our witness at the Ferris wheel," admitted Wannamaker.

"I tried to tell you," said the big man. "I'm the victim here. Look at this –" He indicated a goose-egg knot on his forehead. "I'm injured. I've got a heckuva headache. I'm gonna sue somebody."

"Appears that you were in the wrong place at the wrong time, Mr. Yager." Wannamaker turned to the Police Chief. "You can let him go, Jim."

"Okay, if you say so," acquiesced the Chief, reaching for the keys to the cell.

"You got any idea who attacked me?" asked the big man as he stepped out of the holding cell.

Neil Wannamaker cleared his throat. "We think you ran across the kidnapper," he said.

"Any clue who it is? I've got a score to settle with that joker."

"Mr. Bentley here says it may be a local Indian named Matea Davison."

"Davis," Deputy Hitzer corrected.

"I didn't say it was Matea," responded Ben Bentley. "I just said he knows how to make a wigwam, him being an Indian and all."

"It's hard to believe Matea would do this," remarked Jim Purdue. "N'yen and Aggie adore him."

"Right now, Davis is our main suspect. He fits the profile developed by Special Agent Bradshaw to a T," confirmed Wannamaker. "A male between 18 and 25. Ethnic minority. Someone the boy knows and obviously trusts. Check, check, and check."

"Matea Davis – that's sure a surprise," said Petie Hitzer. "I always pegged him as a good apple."

"You'd have a hard time convincing me of that," groused Hank Yager, rubbing the bump on his head.

~ ~ ~

At that exact moment Edgar Ridenour and Matea Davis walked into the police station with N'yen protectively sandwiched between them. Now that was a showstopper.

"Edgar, you've found him!" Jim Purdue exclaimed, relief in his voice.

"And you've captured the kidnapper too," added Agent Neil Wannamaker, placing a hand on Matea's arm as if to prevent him from running away.

"Hey, I'm no kidnapper," protested Matea. "I am a *memegwesi*."

N'yen looked puzzled. "I thought you said you were a Potawatomi."

"A *memegwesi* is a protector of children," Matea explained under his breath. "Remember, I told you that story."

"Oh yeah. I liked that one. Bearded dwarfs who live in caves by the river."

"*Memegwesi* – my eye," declared Neil the Nailer. "You're the kidnapper who's been holding the boy captive up there in Injun Woods."

"No, no," rumbled Edgar Ridenour, stepping between Matea and the FBI agent. "Matea didn't kidnap N'yen. They merely went camping and forgot to tell anybody. It's all very innocent. "

"Forgot to tell anybody?" said Deputy Hitzer. "That doesn't sound very responsible."

"I left a note," offered Matea Davis.

"A ransom note." Petie hadn't been in on the FBI briefing so he didn't understand the distinctions between a kidnapping and an abduction.

"No," Matea said, just as they'd rehearsed it. "My note didn't ask for any money. It merely assured N'yen's family that he was with me and would be safe."

"Maybe you should have mentioned that you were taking him camping," Agent Wannamaker pointed out.

"Guess I overlooked that," allowed the Native American. "Sorry."

"That might have saved everybody a lot of trouble," grumbled Jim Purdue. "We've been setting up roadblocks and conducting house-to-house searches. And the FBI deployed a dozen men. Not to mention a helicopter that they'll probably try to charge the town for." He was speaking like he'd never retired as the town's chief of police.

"An oversight," shrugged the young man.

"I'll say," snarled the FBI agent, still not satisfied. But he could tell kidnapping charges wouldn't hold up in this case.

"This has been a big misunderstanding," Edgar told his friend Jim. "No harm intended. Just an overnight camping trip as a going-away present to N'yen."

"I had a great time," grinned the small Asian boy. "I hope Matea will take me again."

"Well —"

"I think we better call the boy's family," said a voice from the back of the room – dispatcher Myrtle Dobbler. Myrtle was always the calm one in an emergency. That's what made her a good police dispatcher. She also doubled as the 9-1-1 operator, linking the police department, the fire department, the paramedics, and Burpyville Memorial.

"Do that," nodded Jim Purdue. "I'm sure his parents have been frantic. Beau and Maddy too."

Petie said, "We better shut down all the roadblocks."

"And I'm going to pull the CARD team," sighed Special Agent in Charge Wannamaker.

Ben Bentley took a deep breath. "I'm glad it was a false alarm."

"Me too," said Jim Purdue, ruffling N'yen's raven-black hair in a reassuring manner.

"We're going to miss you, little buddy," said Edgar Ridenour. Looking about to cry.

"I'm going to miss all of you too," said the boy. "But I'll be back. Then we can go fishing —"

"You bet."

"—and Matea and I can go camping again."

"If your parents say it's okay," replied the young Potawatomi. "We don't want to call out the cops again."

"They will. Right, Uncle Edgar?"

The retired bank president gave a feeble nod.

"*Pama mine' o knowabmin*," Matea assured the boy.

"All's well that ends well," smiled Myrtle Dabbler. She loved a happy ending.

"Win some, lose some," Neil Wannamaker shrugged. "At least I'll get a quick ride home in the helicopter."

Jim Purdue said, "Now all I've got to do is figure out who killed Evers Gochnauer."

Chapter Forty-Three

Fingering the Murderer

Upon receiving the news of N'yen's return, Maddy and Beau rushed over to the police department with the boy's parents in tow. Aggie insisted in coming along too; there was no holding her back.

"Oh, thank the Lord," cried Maddy, rushing forward to hug the small boy.

"Aw, Grammy," he wiggled in her grasp.

"We were so worried," said Beau.

"Sorry, Grampy. I didn't mean to upset anybody. Matea and I left a note. The camping trip was a goodbye gift from my goodest friend."

Maddy said, "Hon, you should have asked our permission. Your mom and dad were so worried. So was your Grampy and I."

"Me too!" interjected Aggie.

N'yen gave her a withering look. "Aw, you were busy having a Blizzard with your stupid ol' boyfriend. You didn't care that I was going camping – in a wigwam like a real Indian."

"Native American," corrected Maddy. Always sensitive to terminology.

"Actually, most of us call ourselves Indians," said Matea Davis. Trying to hold back a smile.

"Oh."

The Potawatomi added, "N'yen and I were having a great time until we were attacked by an intruder."

Hank Yager stepped forward. "Hey, I didn't attack you. You attacked me!" he shouted. That caused Deputy Hitzer to step between the two men. There would be no fisticuffs here in the police department.

"Everybody, keep calm," warned Chief Purdue. This might be a temporary job, but he was going to maintain a professional decorum.

"You're the man with the shotgun," accused the Indian. "You almost blasted me."

"That's a lie!"

"*Nde'bwe'*. I speak the truth."

"Matea, how about telling us what happened when you encountered Mr. Yager." Something wasn't right here.

"N'yen and I were having breakfast, about ready to break camp and head home when we heard a noise –"

"Yes, that's what happened," exclaimed the boy.

"N'yen, wait your turn," said his Uncle Jim. Trying not to come across like an authoritarian lawman. But he wanted to get Matea's story without comments from the Peanut Gallery.

"I went toward the mound to investigate, then suddenly this *mjumnito* –" Matea pointed toward the man in the orange jumpsuit. "— jumped me."

"Did not," objected Yager.

Matea plowed on. "Like I said, he tried to shoot me, but I knocked his shotgun aside with my walking stick."

"That's a lie," shouted Yager.

"We did find a shotgun at the scene," Petie Hitzer reminded his boss. "It had been discharged twice, judging from the empty shells."

Hank Yager protested, "I didn't try to shoot anybody. My Mossberg went off accidentally when he knocked it outta my hand."

"Twice?" sneered the deputy.

Ignoring him, Matea continued with his story. "Like I said, this devil grabbed me and locked his arms around me in a bear hug. My ribs are still sore. But I used a few Okichitaw moves to free myself –"

"Okichi-what?" asked Neil Wannamaker.

N'yen couldn't stop himself from interjecting. "Okichitaw – it's an Indian fighting technique. The idea is to move into the attacker's space with a combination of blocks, strikes, holds, and rolls. Matea has shown me some of the moves."

"That's a real fighting style?"

N'yen nodded. "Indians used a form of Okichitaw back in the old days. But it wasn't formally developed as a martial art until 1997. George J. Lépine, a Plains-Cree Michif, combined this native combat skills with judo and taekwondo to create Okichitaw. Now it's recognized as a unique indigenous martial art of Canada by the World Martial Arts Union."

"How do you know all this?" asked the FBI man.

"I read."

Maddy couldn't help but smile at this disquisition by her little genius. The boy was even smarter than Cookie. She merely had a trick memory, but N'yen's IQ was somewhere off the scale.

Kathy Madison looked at her son the way one might view an exotic cryptid. A jackalope, say. Or a unicorn. She barely recognized the cute little Asian boy she and Bill had adopted five years ago.

Not to be sidetracked, Matea Davis continued, "So I freed myself and struck him with my walking stick. Self-defense ... and to protect the boy in my care."

"Then what happened?" coaxed the FBI agent.

"Got outta Dodge. I grabbed N'yen and we escaped in my *ciman* – my canoe."

"Hm," responded the agent. "How did you manage to evade my men?"

The Potawatomi put on an expression of great surprise. "Were your men looking for us? If I'd known help was on the way, we wouldn't have felt the need to run."

Neil the Nailer didn't bother explaining that they had not been there to give him aid; rather, they were on the track of a suspected kidnapper. "So where did you go?" he pressed.

"We paddled down river to a place where Mr. Ridenour picked us up. He and N'yen had arranged a spot to meet in case of an emergency on the river."

Beau spoke up: "That's right, Jim. Edgar and I picked out a place to meet up if we ever got separated while fishing on the river. That abutment under the Highway 101 Bridge."

"That's exactly where I found them," nodded the retired banker. "Beau and I had been out there last night looking for them. I thought I'd give it another try and – *presto!* – they showed up."

"Hmm," said Jim Purdue, rubbing his chin. He vaguely remembered Beau and Edgar telling him about a rendezvous place. A smart safety procedure, he'd thought at the time.

Hank Yager took this opportunity to jump in. "That's not true, Chief. I went up to Injun Woods to retrieve my kid's backpack and this bloodthirsty Redskin attacked me, started beating me with a stick. I didn't do anything to provoke him. He's a dangerous menace. I demand you arrest him!"

"Well, now –" Jim Purdue hesitated.

Ben Bentley felt caught in the middle. He knew and trusted Matea Davis, a frequent participant in his Badger Patrol training sessions. Yet Hank Yager was the father of one of his Badger Patrol boys. "Something's out of whack here," he said, a frown on his face.

"I'll say," Maddy Madison spoke up. "This is the man who murdered Evers Gochnauer."

Chapter Forty-Four
"You Can't Prove That"

Everybody stared at her, shocked at the statement. But Maddy Madison wasn't one to make false accusations.

Chief Jim Purdue was the first to speak. "You're saying Mr. Yager here is a murderer?"

"That's exactly what I'm saying."

Hank Yager shouted, "You can't prove that."

"I think I can," she replied calmly.

"Go ahead, Maddy," said Jim Purdue. By first-hand experience, he knew better than doubt the Quilters Club. "How do you figure this jasper killed Evers?"

"Well –"

"Watch what you say," warned Yager, "or you'll be hearing from my lawyer, J. Harold Wentworth."

Aggie laughed. "Fat chance of that," she said.

Yager turned to her, a scowl on his pock-marked face. "What's so funny about that, young lady?"

"You may have to find a new attorney," she replied blithely, a twinkle in her blue eyes. "Mr. Worthington may be moving far away."

Yager looked puzzled. "Why would he do that?"

"I heard he has fallen out of favor with some important people."

Yager snorted. "And who would that be, pray tell?"

"Salvatore Milano," offered Maddy. "You may have heard of him by his street name, Sal the Whisperer."

"Jeez, that's not good," muttered the big man in the orange jumpsuit.

"Hmm, that's very interesting," said FBI Special Agent in Charge Neil Wannamaker. "Are you sure about that, Mrs. Madison."

"Heard it with my own ears."

"Me too," Aggie added. A bright smile on her face.

"Maddy, what makes you say this guy killed Evers?" coaxed Chief Jim Purdue. Trying to get back to the accusation she'd just made.

"As Bootsie likes to say, Motive, Means, Opportunity."

"Is he a hobo?" asked Beau. Sticking to his pet theory.

Maddy patted her husband on the arm. "No. And he's not an Indian either. But he killed Evers."

"You're sure about this?" asked Chief Purdue. More a plea than a question.

"Yes," said Maddy. "But there's more you need to know." She nodded toward Viola Fahrner, who had been sitting quietly at the police chief's desk. "Hank Yager didn't do it alone. He had some help from your deputy."

Viola's eyes widened as she came to life. "That's a dirty lie," shouted the pretty black woman. "I don't even know that man."

"Now, now, Viola. You and Hank have been having an affair for the past year. Didn't you tell me that you and your boyfriend were celebrating your first anniversary?"

"You can't prove any of this," interjected Hank Yager.

"No, you can't prove it," echoed Viola Fahrner. "We didn't leave no fingerprints."

Maddy smiled at the woman's *faux pas.* "The proof, my dear, is in your Charm quilt."

"Charm quilt? What the heck's a Charm quilt?" asked the FBI man. A quizzical look crossing his craggy face. Having worked around the clock, he was showing pouches under his tired brown eyes and a darkening five o'clock shadow.

"That's a patchwork quilt with no two pieces alike," said Aggie, parroting her Aunt Lizzie's description. Last year Lizzie Ridenour had made a Charm quilt, a laborious undertaking that took First Place at the Watermelon Days quilting competition.

"Oh, I see," said the FBI agent. Not quite understanding.

"Except Viola's masterpiece wasn't really a Charm quilt," corrected Maddy Madison. "It was what's we call an Oddfellow quilt, one that actually has two pieces out of the hundreds that match. Like a puzzle, it's a challenge to find them."

"And you found it?" asked Jim Purdue.

"Of course."

"How does that identify her boyfriend?" asked Neil Wannamaker, caught up in the mystery. He'd never heard of an Oddfellow quilt. For that matter, he'd never heard of a Charm quilt.

"Simple. The matching scraps on Viola's fancy quilt were name patches from Hank Yager's coveralls – HANK and HANK."

Ben frowned. "Hank works at Aitkens Produce. He wears tan coveralls with a big name patch on it. Just his first name, but he's the only Hank out there."

Viola Fahrner sat back down. "Okay, I admit it. Hank's my boyfriend," she sniffed, giving up the pretense. "But that don't prove we killed nobody."

Chapter Forty-Five
The Confession

Maddy fluffed her silver coiffure as she organized her thoughts. Taking a deep breath, she continued, "Here's what happened: Chief Gochnauer got a call on Friday afternoon from Hank's lawyer. Something about his latest accident claim, I expect. Myrtle logged the call."

"That's right," the dispatcher confirmed. "Got it right here in the book."

"Somewhere in that conversation the lawyer let it slip that his client was having a fling with Deputy Fahrner."

"How do you know that?" challenged Hank Yager. "You got a crystal ball or something?"

"I can answer that," said Ben Bentley. "Chief Gochnauer told his cousin Tommy that he was meeting with Viola to head off a scandal. Said she was carrying on with a married man. But at the time nobody knew it was Hank."

"Look, I'd talked to Johnny Wentworth about me filing for a divorce," offered Yager. "There didn't have to be a scandal."

"Hank and I were gonna get married," Viola nodded, a quavering desperation in her voice.

Chief Purdue had been taking all this in. "Here's a theory," he said. "What if Gochnauer threatened to

239

expose them and Hank. Yager killed him in the heat of the moment."

"A very good theory," said Maddy. "Viola Fahrner lives up near Injun Woods. That would've been a convenient place to get rid of a body."

"But how'd he get inside?" repeated Ben Bentley. "I had the only key."

"Apparently not," said Jim Purdue. "He admitted to me and Petie that Elmer Jackson Wayne's lawyer gave him an extra key. He liked to hunt up there in Injun Woods."

"That's true," nodded Matea Davis. "I've seen him skulking around the place on numerous occasions, that big shotgun over his shoulder. He bagged squirrels mostly. Sometimes a *suksi* – a deer."

"Now hold on a minute," bellowed Hank Yager. "Why would I hide a body in the spot where the Badger Patrol would be camping the very next day."

Maddy frowned. "That puzzled me too."

"I can explain that," said Ben Bentley. "You see, I changed the location at the last minute. We were scheduled to camp out at Gruesome Gorge but I got the key to Injun Woods from the lawyer and decided to try out SAW's new property."

"But wouldn't Mr. Yager know about that, since Georgie was going camping with them?" asked Myrtle Dobbler. She didn't usually insert herself into investigations, but this was something of a free-for-all.

"Matter of fact, I did leave a message with Hank's wife," said Ben. "Notified all the parents."

"But she couldn't give her husband the message," Aggie pointed out, "because he and Miss Fahrner were busy killing Chief Gochnauer that night."

"Makes sense," nodded the FBI agent.

"I think you've nailed it," said Chief Purdue.

"Viola, I'm shocked," chastised Deputy Petie Hitzer. "I know I've wanted to kill Evers on dozens of occasions, but at the end of the day I'm a lawman. It's our job to stop crimes, not commit them."

Viola Fahrner cracked. "We didn't mean to kill Evers. Things just got outta control."

"Shut up, Viola. You'll put us both in prison," shouted Hank Yager. His face as red as a ripe watermelon.

"The two of 'em got into a scuffle," sobbed the female deputy. "I hit Evers on the head with a rock and knocked him out. He was unconscious about six or eight hours. When he finally come to, he got all fussy, said he was gonna arrest us. So Hank grabbed a rope from the back of his truck and 'fore you knowed it he'd strangled Evers."

"That explains the Indian rope," said Matea. "His son Georgie made it when I taught the Badger Patrol woodlore techniques."

"And the timing," said Jim Purdue. "Him being knocked out for six hours, that matches. Doc Medford placed the death at about three in the morning."

"You folks may as well let me outta here," called Jeb Crackleton from his holding cell. "You're gonna need this extra room for your deputy."

"Don't be in such a hurry, Mr. Crackleton," responded SAC Neil Wannamaker. "My boys are going to take you back to Indianapolis with us. We have plenty of cells down in Indy."

"Hold on," the tall man protested. "I'm innocent as the lamb of Jesus. I was just taking my nephew for a look at the Bottomless Sinkhole when those crazy women drove up with a bunch of police."

"FBI agents," Neil Wannamaker corrected him.

"Whatever. Your men had enough guns to overthrow a South American country."

"Gee, Mr. Crackleton," said Aggie. "There's one big hole in your story. If you intended to show Gus the Bottomless Sinkhole, why did you have a hood over his head? It's hard to enjoy the sights when you're blindfolded like that."

"Hey, that's pretty smart," said N'yen, forgetting that he was miffed at his cousin.

"Thanks, you shrimp. I'm gonna miss you."

"Me too. I'll come back to visit when I can."

"That might be a very long time," counseled his cousin. "I suspect Uncle Bill's gonna ground you for about a billion years for that overnight camping stunt."

"You've got that right," said Bill Madison. But he didn't sound serious. He was just relieved his son had turned up safe.

"Yes, you're grounded for life," Kathy joined the hyperbola. But with a smile on her face. She was still a little wonky from the Valium.

"Hmph," N'yen sighed. "At least I'll have plenty more time to read."

Then things got very active in the crowded police department. Bill and Kathy hugging N'yen. Beau handing Maddy a handkerchief. Edgar patting Matea

242

reassuringly on the shoulder. Ben shaking hands with Neil the Nailer.

Chief Jim Purdue took charge. "Petie, place Viola and her boyfriend under arrest for the murder of Evers Gochnauer," he instructed. "Hank can go back in his cell; Viola can take Jeb's place. And Jeb will get a ride to Indy with the Feds."

"You bet, Chief," said Petie. Turning to his fellow deputy, he said, "I'm sorry to hafta do this, Viola. I always liked you."

"Go ahead, Petie," she sniffled. "Lock me up. I deserve it. Never should've got mixed up with a married man in the first place."

"Hey," whined Hank Yager. "I really was gonna divorce my wife for you."

"Yeah, you kept saying that, but you never did," she retorted. "Now look what you got me into."

"Ah, Poopsie –"

"Don't you Poopsie me, you homicidal maniac. I'm gonna spent the next 40 years in prison just 'cause you can't hold your temper."

Petie Hitzer shook his head sadly. "That's not why you're going to jail, Viola. It's because you helped your boyfriend kill Evers Gochnauer. You hit him on the head with a rock. You tried to hide the body. You're as guilty as Hank."

"Evers deserved it," she pouted. "He was mean to me, a big bully. He threatened to fire me."

Petie shook his head. "That's no excuse. I didn't like him much myself, but he *was* our Chief."

Epilogue

Like with many of these stories, the bad guys went to jail.

For instance, former mayor Henry Caruthers was arrested when he and Nan Beanie showed up at the Pleasant Glades caretaker's cottage to pick up her mother's ruby ring. Based on Cookie Bentley's tip, SAC Neil Wannamaker had stationed an FBI agent there. Henry Caruthers had not exactly been on the Top Ten Wanted List, but he was still a good catch. The Feds hated having loose ends and unclosed cases. Ol' Henry was sentenced to five years in Joliet; Nan got off with a two-year probation.

As for Jebediah Crackleton, he received ten years at Indiana State Prison. Extortion and child trafficking are serious charges in Indiana. He was on the same cell block as his son Dub. They made an odd pair – one nearly seven feet tall, the other a dwarf. Fellow inmates referred to them as the "long and the short of it."

~ ~ ~

Ten-year-old Gus Ritchie – Jeb's nephew – was disappointed that he didn't get sold to those nice ladies in the Quilters Club. They were wealthy, he'd heard. Truth was, he didn't like living with his mother in Crackleton Crossing. Most of the people there were weirdos with strange deformities: Lobster hands. Vestigial tails. Extra fingers. Cleft palates. Small heads (microcephaly, whatever that was). Conjoined twins.

What some people called a Hapsburg Jaw. Even Gus had webs between his toes like a lizard.

But things changed: Now running the convenience store in her brother Jeb's forced absence, Faith Ann Ritchie agreed to let Family Services place three of her children in foster homes, domiciles that would provide a better environment than Crackleton Crossing. As it happened, Cookie and Ben took in Gus. Being a 60ish couple past the childbearing age, they had wanted a youngster of their own.

Gus liked his new home. And he liked going to a new school. If he kept his shoes on, nobody would know he was a Crackleton.

~ ~ ~

With Mayor Mark Tidemore's urging, Jim Purdue agreed to stay on for another term as police chief. His wife Bootsie encouraged him to accept the offer. He'd been driving her nuts hanging around the house with nothing to do. He was happiest when solving crimes – even with the Quilters Club's uninvited assistance.

And – yes – N'yen went back to Chicago with Bill and Kathy, vowing to visit his grandparents often. He figured the Quilters Club could use his help in solving crimes. And he had to admit he'd miss his cousin Aggie, even if she was spending most her time with that jerk Bobby Elwood.

N'yen's online gaming nemesis Beelzebub666 – Tommy Truehart, that is – promised to stay in touch, the two of them looking forward to many more Tower Defense battles in the future.

Tommy was credited with the "rescue" of the young Asian friend he'd never met face-to-face. As a reward for his civic responsibility, Chief Purdue hired him as a deputy. The police department was shorthanded, what with Evers dead and Viola Fahrner doing 40 years for murder.

Hank Yager was doing 40 years too. The judge said he wished Indiana law allowed him to give Yager and his accomplice longer sentences, but that was the max allowed. The prison psychiatrist diagnosed Yager as being given to fits of irrational anger. Intermittent Explosive Disorder, it was called. His new lawyer filed an appeal based on "cognitive impairment," but it wasn't going anywhere.

Emily Yager filed for divorce. Nobody was surprised.

Edgar Ridenour never admitted that he was the mastermind behind N'yen Madison's "kidnapping." But he was pretty sure his wife suspected. He and Beau continued to go fishing every weekend. They both missed their little fishing buddy.

Matea Davis kept his mouth shut too. He gave up his job as night watchman at the Industrial Park, taking Tommy Truehart's old position as stock boy at Dollar General. That freed him up so he could become Ben Bentley's replacement as the Badger Patrol's troop leader. Ben had been appointed CEO of Sons of Anthony Wayne. The headquarters would be moving from Indy to Caruthers Corners, another feather in Mayor Tidemore's cap. The population – and town's tax base – was slowly growing.

Aggie was blossoming into a lovely young woman. She and Bobby Elwood were going steady. But she missed her cousin N'yen. They were like a mismatched pair of Bobbsey Twins. They kept in touch by telephone.

Maddy and her Quilters Club friends started a project for National Quilting Day. The annual event always took place on the third Thursday in March, but the girls needed to get a head start. Maddy had proposed that they involve the whole town in making a scrap quilt that would cover the Town Square – 10 acres in all. Quite an undertaking. She was sure it would make the Guinness Book of World Records.

Aggie looked it up: The current record holder was a 270,174 sq. ft. patchwork quilt in Portugal. Called Manta da Cultura (Patchwork for Culture), it had been completed in June 2000 by Realizar Eventos Especiais of Parque da Cidade, Porto. That was 6.2 acres – only two-thirds the size of the Town Square.

The Caruthers Corners Friendship Quilt – as they'd decided to call it – was sure to take the title.

However, as it happened, that ambitious project got sidetracked when a violent EF3 tornado ripped through Caruthers Corners with wind speeds of 150 MPH, destroying two-thirds of the town and rendering the Madison family homeless. In all, 37 people died. And a famous quilt – Marie Webster's 1927 "Pink Dogwoods in Appliqué" – went missing. You may have read about this in the newspapers. If not, we will tell you that story in the next book.

● ● ●

End Notes

These footnotes identify the Quilters Club book(s) where Maddy, Bootsie, Lizzie, and Cookie first encountered the villains on their list of suspects in this story.

1. The Crackletons – *Cross Stitch, Fat Quarters*
2. The Mob – *Sewed Up Tight, All Tangled Up, Needled, Fat Quarters*
3. Horace Greeley -- *Fat Quarters*
4. Casper Crane – *Fat Quarters*
5. Maurey Siederman – *Hemmed In, Fat Quarters*
6. Jason Perricock – *A Stitch in Time*
7. Max Kasper – *All Tangled Up*
8. The Russians -- *Needled*
9. Henry Caruthers – *The Underhanded Stitch, The Patchwork Quilt*
10. Stanley Caruthers – *Sewed Up Tight*
11. Bern Bjorn – *Hemmed In*
12. The Blickensderfer brothers -- *A Stitch in Time*

Thank you for reading. Please review this book.
Reviews help others find Absolutely Amazing eBooks
and inspire us to keep providing these marvelous
tales. If you would like to be put on our email list to
receive updates on new releases, contests,
and promotions, please go to
AbsolutelyAmazingEbooks.com and sign up.

Bonus

If you go to the Absolutely Amazing eBooks online bookstore (AbsolutelyAmazingEbooks.com) and enter the password below into the Bonus Reward Section, you can access recipes for many of the dishes you read about in this book – for free!

AA1060

About the Author

Marjory Sorrell Rockwell says needlecraft arts – quilting, crocheting, knitting – are pastimes every woman can appreciate. And she particularly loves quilt making. "It's like painting with cloth," she says. But when not quilting she writes mysteries about a Midwestern sleuth not unlike herself, a middle-aged lady with an unpredictable family and loyal friends. And she's a big fan of watermelon pie.

ABSOLUTELY AMAZING eBOOKS

AbsolutelyAmazingeBooks.com
or AA-eBooks.com

www.ingramcontent.com/pod-product-compliance
Lightning Source LLC
Chambersburg PA
CBHW071828020726
47502CB00004B/1284